"I've been wanting to do this all evening."

There was raw passion in Joe's voice, and his fingers trembled as he slowly pulled Libby's silk bodice downward. Then his tongue was tracing her soft curves....

Libby curled her fingers in his hair, trying to tug him closer. She wanted to feel his hot mouth, to have his hard body pressed against her.... "Please stop!" Her whimpered plea escaped through clenched teeth.

Joe's teasing lips moved up her throat until his warm breath was tantalizing her ear. "You want me to stop kissing you?" he whispered in disbelief.

"No!" she moaned urgently. "I want you to stop driving me crazy and make love to me."

Judith McWilliams has her hands full these days settling into a new home in New York State, but she still manages to keep up with her busy writing schedule. Wife, mother of four and one-time teacher, Judith has established herself as a talented and prolific author.

Judith's special brand of humor makes *In Good Faith* a totally enjoyable read. It's her second charming Temptation, and there are more to come in the future!

Books by Judith McWilliams

HARLEQUIN TEMPTATION
78–POLISHED WITH LOVE

In Good Faith

JUDITH McWILLIAMS

Harlequin Books

TORONTO • NEW YORK • LONDON
AMSTERDAM • PARIS • SYDNEY • HAMBURG
STOCKHOLM • ATHENS • TOKYO • MILAN

To Mary Sittler—
a friend in need.

Published April 1986

ISBN 0-373-25203-X

Printed in Canada

PROLOGUE

"HAVE SOME MORE GOLDWASSER, Sigismund." Casimir Blinkle accepted the bottle from the waiter and poured the golden liquor into his friend's empty glass.

"You *do* look like you need a drink." Frederic Landowski's faded blue eyes studied Sigismund's lined face.

"What I need is a magician!" Sigismund snorted. "Today is my Libby's thirtieth birthday." He shook his head in disbelief. "It hardly seems possible that my little girl is thirty already."

"Congratulations." Casimir gravely raised his glass. "To Libby's continued good health."

"Better to drink to her finding a husband," Sigismund said morosely. "Thirty years old today and she's not even engaged yet. Or likely to be. She spends all her time either teaching or researching mathematical treatises. How does she expect to meet anyone if she's forever buried in her work?" Sigismund threw up his hands in disgust.

"I wonder where she learned to do that, Professor Michalowski?" Casimir asked slyly.

"That's different!" Sigismund exploded. "I'm a man. A man is expected to work and work hard, but a woman's different. Work is something a woman does until she marries and has a family. At the rate Libby's going, I'm never going to have any grandchildren."

"I know exactly what you mean." Frederic nodded his silvery head in commiseration. "My Joseph is thirty-six. Thirty-six and he still has girlfriends!" He spat the word out as if it tasted bad. "And such girlfriends." He rolled his eyes expressively. "Not the type of woman one takes home to meet the family. I keep telling him that all the good girls are being snapped up. But does he listen? No, not my son. He knows it all. Not that he isn't very good at business," Frederic admitted, his very real pride in his son's business acumen flashing through. "He's doubled our company's sales since I retired last year and more than tripled our profits. But making money isn't everything." He recalled his grievance. "Who does he think he's going to leave it to when he's as old as I am? Bah!" He threw his napkin down in disgust, impatiently waving away the waiter when he came to see if anything was the matter. "Just the thought of what I'm missing by my son's selfish refusal to marry and have a family gives me heartburn."

"True, my nine grandchildren are a source of unending delight to me in my retirement," Casimir replied smugly, ignoring the sour glances the other two gave him. "You know," he continued thoughtfully, "it's too bad, in a case like this, there isn't a modern-day equivalent of the Jewish marriage broker. In the old country, if Jewish families had this sort of problem, they'd just hire the matchmaker to negotiate a contract, and that would be the end of it."

"Would that this were the good old days," Frederic lamented.

"Why not?" Sigismund demanded.

"Why not what?" Casimir blinked in confusion at his friend.

"Why not do it anyway?" Sigismund elaborated. "I know this is the eighties instead of the twenties and it's New York City instead of the Chocholowska Valley, but we can still borrow the basic idea." He turned in excitement to the puzzled-looking Frederic. "You have a son of good character—"

"Mostly," Frederic interrupted, but Sigismund ignored him.

"And I have a daughter in good health with a spotless reputation, and Casimir here, surely knows how to negotiate a contract. You can make an offer to my daughter on behalf of your son."

"Hmm." A gleam of interest appeared in Frederic's eyes.

"Are you two serious?" Casimir glanced from one engrossed face to the other.

"Yes." Sigismund nodded emphatically. "Desperate situations call for desperate measures."

"He's right." Frederic turned to Casimir. "And we've certainly tried everything else. I swear I've introduced my son to every single woman under forty that I know. I've ordered, pleaded, reasoned, begged and even prayed over him. All to no avail. He goes his merry way and I'm left without the comfort of grandchildren to brighten my old age."

"But you can't seriously expect your children to honor a contract the two of you make," Casimir pointed out, his legal background showing briefly.

"Of course not," Sigismund agreed, "but, perhaps, simply the fact that we've made it will shock them into examining their unnatural life-styles."

"We can always hope," Frederic said without any real conviction in his voice.

"It's almost as if the three of us were fated to meet at that reception at the Polish embassy last month. I with an unmarried daughter and you—" he turned to Frederic "—with an unmarried son, and you—" he gestured toward Casimir "—with the memory of how to bring them together."

"The devil as well as God arranges fate, my friend," Casimir said dryly.

"You can't back out," Sigismund insisted. "Where's your sense of adventure?"

"Right up there beside my fear of being sued for invasion of privacy."

"Bah, you're an old woman!" Frederic scoffed.

"I'm an old judge," Casimir corrected. "An old conservative judge."

"Who already has nine grandchildren." Sigismund sighed.

"I'm not susceptible to emotional blackmail," Casimir shot back.

"What are you susceptible to?"

"Boredom, the same as you two. Life seems to have lost a lot of its zest since I retired and, I will admit, playing matchmaker sounds like the most interesting idea I've heard in months. And, as you pointed out, we do have a Christian duty to try to help your children see the error of their ways."

"You'll help?" Sigismund pressed.

"Yes." An anticipatory smile teased Casimir's thin lips. "But we'll do this thing in style. I should be able to get a period costume from my youngest son who's a Broadway producer."

"A costume?" Frederic questioned. "Is that necessary?"

"Absolutely," Casimir insisted. "The right costume predisposes people to react in predictable ways. Why do you think policemen wear uniforms or judges wear robes?"

"We'll just have to hope Libby's seen *Fiddler on the Roof*," Sigismund said dryly, too grateful for his friend's cooperation to contest the matter.

"It's settled then?" Sigismund looked at his two friends. "We'll write a contract and Casimir will present it to Libby."

"Yes." Frederic lifted his glass. "To success in the form of at least six grandchildren."

"To success," Sigismund and Casimir echoed happily.

1

"IS THAT THE DOORBELL?" Libby brushed a blond-streaked curl behind her ear, cocked her head and listened.

"It's probably your neighbors come to threaten you with the police." Jessie Anders laughed.

"Not a chance." Libby's answering grin illuminated her bright blue eyes. "I was very careful to invite them all to the party. Besides, we aren't making that much noise." She glanced around complacently at the small clusters of people packed into her living room. If the intensity of the conversation was any sign, her combined end-of-term thirtieth-birthday party was a roaring success.

"I'd better check." Libby began to weave her way through the chattering groups. She paused a second in front of the door to adjust the waistband of her long black silk skirt before reaching for the doorknob.

Her welcoming smile slipped slightly as she took in the apparition in front of her. A short thin man of at least seventy, dressed in a rusty-black threadbare suit. A slightly crushed black felt hat was clutched in one gnarled hand, while several sheets of paper were held in his other hand.

Libby thought she detected a flicker of dismay cross his face as he took in the party behind her, but it was gone so quickly, she wasn't sure. The man seemed to draw on an inborn hauteur; he radiated authority.

Libby automatically responded to it.

"May I help you, sir?" she asked, wondering what he was doing there. From the looks of his suit, he'd be hard-pressed to pay for a good square meal, let alone the relatively modest rent charged for apartments in this building.

"Are you Liberty Joy Michalowski, spinster?" His stentorian tones rolled into the room behind her, crushing conversation as they went.

"Yes."

"Then allow me to present you with a formal proposal of marriage."

Libby stared at the man in dumbfounded amazement. She opened her mouth, but no sound escaped. Clearing her throat, she tried again.

"Marriage?" she squeaked. "You're asking me to marry you?"

A gleam of wicked amusement flared in his black eyes only to be quickly banished.

"Alas, dear lady." He sighed theatrically, "alluring as you undoubtedly are, I fear you can not seduce me from my wife of fifty-one years. No, you see before you a simple emissary from the bridegroom." He handed her the papers he was holding.

"Allow me to be the first to offer you sincere felicitations for having captured the attention of one Joseph Landowski."

Libby automatically took the papers he was holding out to her.

The old man gave her a courtly bow, turned on his heel and marched off down the hall.

Libby watched in mesmerized fascination as he stepped into the elevator and disappeared from sight. Shaking her head as if to repudiate what had just happened, she turned to find herself the focus of all eyes.

"Libby Michalowski, spinster!" Frank Lessing, a fellow math professor at Columbia, whom she'd always rather liked until that moment, guffawed. "Now I've heard everything."

"If you don't shut up, you'll find you haven't heard anything yet." Jessie poked him in the ribs.

"That I should live to hear the light of the math department stigmatized as a spinster!" Frank continued to chortle, a sound that grated over Libby's nerve endings.

"Who on earth was that character?" someone asked. "He looked like he was on his way to a dress rehearsal for a Broadway play."

"He didn't introduce himself." Libby forced an even tone, determined not to let this extraordinary event ruin her party. At least for her. Her friends seemed to be finding the man's visit the highlight of the evening. She glanced around the room, registering the looks of avid curiosity and sympathy for her embarrassment, all overlaid by amusement.

She was never going to live this down, Libby realized with a sinking feeling of helplessness. It was much too priceless an anecdote not to become a classic. She would probably still be hearing about it when she was as old as the messenger had been.

"Are you going to accept?" Betty, a secretary in the math department, asked.

"What's he willing to pay for a bride of such skills?" Frank quipped. "After all, female Ph.D.s with Phi Beta Kappa's in math are rather thin on the ground."

"Careful, Frank—" Libby gave him a tight smile "—or we might begin to think you're jealous."

"Damn right I'm jealous." Frank was unperturbed at her charge. "It just isn't natural for a woman to be so good in math. Math is a man's field."

"Unlike tact." Jessie handed him a glass of wine. "Here. Be quiet and drink this before you say anything you're going to regret."

"You know, Libby, they used to propose marriage in much the same way in the African tribe I worked with when I was in the peace corps," Dave Talbot, a brand-new lecturer in sociology, observed. "The village elder would offer so many cows to the bride on behalf of the bridegroom's family."

"Cows!" Betty choked on her drink. "Whatever happened to cold, hard cash?"

"Cows are a form of cash among certain tribes," Dave insisted.

Frank snickered. "How many cows would you say Libby was worth?"

Libby bit down on the bubbling anger filling her, well aware that showing she was upset would be fatal. There were times when her normally well-mannered friends reminded her of a group of three-year-olds, and unruly ones at that.

"I'd give two cows just to have Libby's curly blond hair," Betty said with good-natured envy.

"And that flawless complexion," someone piped up from the back of the room.

"To say nothing of her glorious body." Frank leered playfully at her. "I'd give my whole herd for her."

"You're getting carried away with the animal analogy." Libby forced a smile. "You sound like a pack of wolves."

"Want to go bay at the moon with me?" Frank wiggled his eyebrows in a hopeless parody of Groucho Marx.

"Okay, you've all had your laugh." Jessie rescued her friend. "Come on, Libby, we need to get some more ice cubes."

"Sure." Libby smiled gratefully at Jessie and followed her into the kitchen, the papers still clutched in her hand.

"WELL?" Frederic and Sigismund demanded the second Casimir stepped out of the elevator and into the lobby. "So how did it go?"

"As battle tacticians, you two belong on the other side," Casimir said in disgust.

"What does that mean?" Frederic frowned. "All you had to do was deliver the contract. What kind of planning does that take?"

"She was having a party." Casimir explained, enlightening them.

Sigismund winced. "Oh!"

"Yes, 'oh.' We had an audience Neilson wouldn't have scorned."

"Was she mad?" Sigismund asked.

"She hadn't made it to mad yet. She was still in the disbelieving stage when I left. I haven't seen anyone that dumbfounded since I slapped a contempt of court on that foulmouthed attorney from Queens last year." His eyes lit up briefly with remembered pleasure. "But you mark my words—" Casimir impaled his fellow conspirators with a grim look "—when the initial shock fades, she's going to come looking for blood."

"Not mine," Frederic said with unconcealed relief. "She doesn't know who I am."

"Nor me," Casimir said as the two turned to look at Sigismund.

"I think I'll take her mother to Atlantic City for the weekend," Sigismund hastily planned. "All that can happen there is that I lose my wallet. Here I could lose my head."

"A wise decision," Casimir agreed. "Now let's go get a drink. Matchmaking is a thirsty business."

LIBBY SLAMMED THE EMPTY ICE BUCKET on the Formica countertop and rubbed her forehead.

"Be calm," Jessie advised. "Think of your blood pressure."

"What I'm thinking about is the pleasure I'm going to derive from slowly choking this . . . this . . ." She waved a slender hand toward the papers she'd dropped on the counter.

"Joseph Landsowski," Jessie read.

"Then I think I'll beat him to a pulp," Libby continued ghoulishly.

"Whoa, girl. He might be bigger than you are."

"I'm five-eight."

Jessie looked slightly confused.

"So he can't be taller?"

"Allow me to describe Joseph Landowski," Libby gritted. "He's approximately five-six, very slender, very nervous and extremely shy. When addressed by members of the opposite sex, he gulps and whispers either 'yes, ma'am' or 'no, ma'am' to every conversational gambit tried."

"You've met Joseph Landowski?"

"I didn't have to meet him. I recognize my father's fine hand in this." Libby grimaced. "Joseph Landowski is obviously one of the young political refugees from Poland my father is helping to get established."

"Why would your father engineer something like this?"

"It's simple." Libby sighed. "Pathetically simple, really. Dad wants to see me respectably married with a brood of kids. He's been trying to interest me in one of his lame ducks for years. Only this time he's chosen a more original approach."

"It certainly got your attention."

"And everyone else's," Libby said gloomily.

"You know, there was something about that old guy, though." Jessie tugged a brown curl thoughtfully.

"Maybe you ran across him in a courtroom on a vagrancy charge."

"Don't laugh. I have the strangest feeling I've seen him before."

"In a nightmare?" Libby suggested dryly.

"It was when he looked down his nose at you." Jessie frowned. "That inbred, 'damn your eyes' arrogance was vaguely familiar."

"Well, let me know when you manage to figure it out and I'll add him to my hit list," Libby said, knowing that Jessie would continue to worry the subject until eventually she'd remember. Her unbelievable tenacity was part of what made Jessie such a good lawyer.

"Hurry up with that ice, cowgirl." Frank stuck his head around the door and then hastily withdrew it when he saw the expression on Libby's face.

"Go ahead," Jessie advised the fuming Libby. "I could probably get you off with a plea of justifiable homicide."

"Oh, hell!" Libby groaned as she swung open the freezer door. "I don't believe any of this."

"So what are you going to do?" Jessie watched Libby deftly twist the ice trays into the container.

"I'm going to grit my teeth and smile through all the teasing, and then I'm going to find this Joseph Landowski at number 4 East Seventy-second Street and make him wish he'd never had an amorous impulse in his life."

"Where?"

"How do I know where he has his amorous impulses!"

"No," Jessie said impatiently. "I mean the address. Where did you say this Landowski character lives?"

"Four East Seventy-second Street, apartment 11-D." Libby's pale pink nail pointed to the typewritten contract.

"A few months back I represented a lady who lived in that building and, let me tell you, unless your immigrant smuggled out St. Stephen's crown, he can't be there."

"Oh, the apartment undoubtedly belongs to an out-of-town friend of my dad's who's letting this Landowski house-sit until he finds his feet," Libby hypothesized. "It's happened before. Dad has a very catholic collection of friends."

"I can imagine. Remember that article about him in *Time* a few years back? They called him one of the intellectual giants of the twentieth century."

"I think senility has just overtaken him."

"Senility tends to be hereditary," Jessie reminded her. "Make sure that you get the facts before you do anything you'll regret."

"I've already got the facts—" Libby gestured toward the contract "—and I most definitely regret the whole mess."

"HERE YOU ARE, LADY. Four East Seventy-second Street. Ritzy neighborhood, ain't it?" The cabbie's eyes lingered doubtfully on the worn denims hugging Libby's slender legs and the oversize, tattered gray sweatshirt enveloping her slight curves. "That'll be four-ten." He held out a beefy hand.

"Keep the change." Libby gave him a five and climbed out of the cab onto the sidewalk, not even noticing his interest. Her concentration was centered on the upcoming confrontation with Joseph Landowski. Her lips thinned at the memory of her guests' laughter. Joseph Landowski was about to receive a crash course in the prevailing courtship customs of modern-day America.

"Have a nice night, lady. At least, what's left of it." He squinted doubtfully at the small green digital clock stuck to his dashboard.

"You, too," Libby responded perfunctorily as the taxi pulled away. Peering through the gleaming glass doors of the luxurious apartment building, she frowned thoughtfully. The understated elegance of the well-lit lobby served to reinforce her initial impression of discreet wealth. As did the burly security guard sitting at the reception desk beside the elevator.

Damn! She swore silently, frustrated. In her hurry to confront Joseph Landowski she'd forgotten to take into account the fact that a building of the type Jessie had described would undoubtedly have a security system, complete with guard.

She stepped back into the shadows out of sight of the doors and considered this unexpected obstacle standing between her and Joseph Landowski.

It would be impossible to sneak past the guard, she conceded. From his vantage point, he had a clear view of anyone entering the lobby. Perhaps a phone call to draw him away.... The idea dawned only to be discarded when a quick peek through the glass doors revealed a phone on his desk. He wouldn't have to move to answer it.

Maybe a delivery, she mused. Say a pizza? She could find an all-night pizza place, get a take-out order, bring it back here and tell the guard that it was for Joseph Landowski. And the guard would use the phone on his desk to call Landowski and check that he'd really ordered it before letting her upstairs; the obvious pitfall of her scheme occurred to her almost immediately.

Pensive, Libby leaned back against the rough brick of the building and tried to push her tired mind to come up with a feasible plan. She was an intelligent, resourceful woman, she thought, giving herself encouragement. Surely she could manage to outwit one lone security guard. But her mind remained discouragingly blank.

Finally she gave up, deciding that the pizza delivery was her only idea that had any chance of success. She'd just have to hope that Joseph Landowski would not only be groggy at having been woken at this late hour but would also be less than fluent in English.

Libby had moved away from the wall to go in search of a restaurant when a cab pulled up beside the next building and an elegantly dressed man of about sixty-five emerged. She watched curiously as he carefully negotiated the curb and then paused to peer uncertainly at the apartment building beside her.

"May I help you," she automatically responded to the confused look on his face.

He squinted doubtfully into the shadow, his eyes brightening when he saw her.

"Yes," he said simply.

Libby waited for him to elaborate, and when he didn't, she tried again.

"What seems to be the problem, sir?"

"I am lost. I wish to go home," he replied with drunken precision.

"Where's home?" she ventured, rather liking him in spite of his obvious inebriation.

"The Meadows."

"Flushing?"

"No. War . . . Warwi . . . England," he amended when he couldn't get out the right word.

"You *are* lost." Libby swallowed a laugh. "You're in New York City."

"That's right. A New York conference. Terrible place," he confided. "No grass."

"There's Central Park," she said, automatically defending her beloved city.

"Where?" He looked around. "I want to see the grass."

"Tomorrow. It's closed now," she hastily improvised, shuddering at the thought of the kind of attention a drunk wearing a thousand-dollar suit and a huge diamond stickpin might attract in the park at this hour of the night.

"Oh." He looked crushed and she felt sorry for him.

"Listen, my friend . . ."

"Fortesque. Peregrine Fortesque," he inserted, and Libby marveled at his diction. She'd always thought drunks slurred their words.

"Mr. Fortesque," she continued, "I think the best thing for you to do would be to go home and go to bed." And sleep it off, she added silently. "Now where's home?"

"I told you, The Meadows."

"No," she said in exasperation. "I meant where are you staying while in New York City?"

"Ah." He nodded sagely. "I remember. An apartment. I hate hotels," he disclosed.

"Very good," Libby said encouragingly. "Which apartment building?"

"Which?" He twisted the end of his gray mustache.

"Yes, which? There are literally hundreds of thousands of apartments in the city. Which one is yours?"

"None," he replied vehemently. "I wouldn't own an apartment in New York City. Ghastly place. No grass."

Libby, with a patience honed by years of teaching graduate students, persisted, "You said you were staying in an apartment."

"Yes." He nodded agreeably, "but it's not mine. The company rented it for me to stay at during the conference."

"Excellent, and where is this apartment the company rented for you?"

"I don't remember." He looked desolate.

"Well, don't worry," she soothed. "I'll think of something." But what? she wondered.

"We could look," he suggested, when her tired mind failed to come up with a practical idea.

"Look?"

"At the address of the apartment."

"You have the address written down!"

"Of course." He seemed surprised at her vehement reaction.

"Then look!" she said in exasperation.

"Really," he muttered as he searched his coat pockets. "The younger generation is always in such a hurry." He extracted a card and peered at it myopically.

"May I?" Libby held out her hand. At the rate this was going she would never get her pizza. And then again, maybe she wouldn't need it! A burst of excitement exploded within her as she read the address engraved on the card. "Four East Seventy-second Street, apartment 6-F." Perfect—she chortled to herself gleefully. All she had to do was deliver Mr. Fortesque to his front door and then continue on up to Landowski's apartment. This plan had a much better chance of success than her idea of pretending to deliver a pizza.

"I'll see you to your door, Mr. Fortesque." She gently took his arm and urged him toward the right building.

"Very decent of you, miss." He obediently followed her lead.

"Not at all." Libby opened the gleaming glass doors into the lobby and, breathing a silent prayer, urged Mr. Fortesque toward the elevator.

"Good evening, Mr. Fortesque," the security guard greeted. "How did your meeting go?"

"Bah!" he snorted in disgust. "The strong dollar's a bloody curse. Hard to afford anything."

"Yes, I can see." The guard's skeptical gaze wandered over Libby's shapeless, tattered sweatshirt.

She gritted her teeth and swallowed a furious retort. His insinuation didn't matter, she told herself. What mattered was that she was about to get her hands on Joseph Landowski.

"Have a good night, Mr. Fortesque." The guard's snicker followed them into the huge carpeted elevator.

Libby let out her breath on a long sigh as the doors slid shut behind them. She'd done it! She was past the guard. Now all she had to do was to deliver Mr. Fortesque to his apartment and she was free to locate Joseph Landowski.

Five minutes later, she stepped off the elevator on the eleventh floor and glanced down the deserted corridor. She pulled the infamous contract out of her pocket and double-checked the apartment number.

"Eleven," she read, turning to the right. She quickly located it.

Libby stared at the wide ivory paneled door of 11-D, feeling her anger beginning to freshen. Behind that door lurked Joseph Landowski who, with the help of her misguided father, had managed to turn her into a laughingstock among her colleagues. It seemed to Libby that the echo of this evening's teasing laughter still floated in the air. The memory stiffened her resolve.

First, she was going to pulverize Joseph Landowski, and then she was going to have it out with her father once and for all. Simply because he loved her did not give him the right to try to arrange her life to suit his own ideas of what she should be doing.

Libby pushed back the voluminous sleeve of her sweatshirt and glanced at her watch: two-ten. Joseph Landowski would undoubtedly be asleep at ten after two. At least, she certainly hoped so. Waking him up was going to give her a great deal of satisfaction.

Libby rapped sharply on the gleaming panel and then rocked back on her heels and waited . . . in vain. Nothing happened. Apparently Joseph Landowski was a heavy sleeper.

"All right, my friend," she muttered as she leaned on the doorbell, keeping her fingers firmly pressed down. Faintly, from within, she could hear its continuous, muted buzz.

A full minute later, the door was jerked open by a gorgeous redhead lavishly dressed in an emerald-green silk evening gown that was obviously haute couture. Surprised, Libby released the doorbell and frowned slightly at the girl. No, woman, she reassessed her initial judgment. In the reflected light of the hallway, the faint lines around the woman's eyes and mouth were visible. As was most everything else. Libby studied her with interest. A rumpled cloud of silky red hair framed exquisitely beautiful features and topped a body that matched the face. Libby's eyes skimmed over the woman's white shoulders and magnificent swell of her creamy breasts exposed by her deeply cut neckline. Swallowing a faint feeling of envy at such a lavish display of nature's attributes, Libby slipped past the woman into the apartment.

"I'd like to see Joseph Landowski," she stated firmly.

"Joey isn't available." The woman frowned, dismissing Libby. "He's in the shower. The champagne sprayed all over him when he tried to open it," she added when Libby didn't move.

That sounded like the Joseph Landowski she'd imagined, Libby thought with satisfaction. Even if the redhead didn't seem to fit in with her preconceived notion.

"Nonetheless, I have to see him. Now."

"What for?" the woman demanded petulantly. "For crying out loud, it's…" She glanced around as if looking for a clock.

"Two-ten." Libby derived a brief flash of pleasure at the woman's annoyed expression. "Now please tell 'Joey' that I'm here to discuss his marriage proposal with him."

"His what?" The redhead's voice rose in a shriek.

"Marriage proposal," Libby obligingly repeated. "His formal, written—" she gestured with the contract "—proposal of marriage."

"Let me see that!" The woman grabbed the contract and skimmed it.

"Why that rat!" The woman flung the papers down on the hall's black marble floor. "That creep!"

Libby blinked, rather amazed at the extent of the woman's fury.

"Romancing me while he's proposing marriage to you!" She gnashed her perfect white teeth. "You wait here. You're welcome to what's left once I'm through with him." With those ominous words, she spun around and stalked off, rage emanating from every rigid line of her body.

Libby reached down and picked up the scattered contract from the floor. Thoughtfully she glanced down the hallway where the woman had disappeared. Presumably it led to the bedrooms and Joseph Landowski. Libby briefly considered following her before deciding against it. She'd wait for Landowski to come to her. As furious as the redhead had been, it wouldn't be long before he came charging out. Provided, of course, he could charge anywhere once his girlfriend vented her ire on him. Libby hoped the woman went easy on him. She wanted the pleasure of demolishing him all for herself.

She hesitated a minute, openly trying to eavesdrop, but the apartment's thick walls muffled all sounds and the only thing she could hear was an indistinct stream of murmurs. Shrugging, Libby moved out of the small foyer and into the huge living room. Surely his proposal of marriage gave her some rights. Such as the one to make herself at home. Not that this was Joseph Landowski's home, she reminded herself. But whoever it belonged to had exquisite taste. She paused in front of a large oil painting that was strongly reminiscent of a Jackson Pollock. She leaned closer, whistling as she read the signature. Exquisite taste *and* the means to indulge them.

"Don't you 'Myrna darling' me, you . . . you . . . licentious philanderer!"

Libby swung around in time to see the redhead storming down the hallway. She was followed by a man wearing a confused expression on his face and not much else.

Libby gasped, unable to tear her eyes away from him. He was huge, overwhelmingly so. At least six-four, possibly more, with a build that a Jets linebacker would have envied. Libby gulped as her eyes measured the intimidating breadth of his well-muscled shoulders. He reached an arm out toward the fuming redhead, and Libby watched in fascination as his biceps rippled beneath his supple skin. As if compelled, her gaze returned to his broad chest, which was covered with a thick pelt of dark blond hair. Involuntarily her eyes traced the curly hair as it arrowed down over his flat stomach to disappear beneath the small towel he held loosely clutched around his narrow hips. With a will of its own, her attention homed in on that scrap of pale green material, which seemed woefully inadequate when measured against the vast amount of tanned skin. For a fugitive second a spark of sexual excitement blazed to life deep within her, but the shrill sound of Myrna's voice doused it, returning Libby to sanity.

What on earth was the matter with her? All but drooling over some virtually naked blond giant. She had never placed a great deal of importance on a man's physical appearance and she wasn't about to start now. Not with this man. The remembrance of this evening's fiasco brought all her antagonism rushing to the fore.

"Myrna, what are you talking about?" He ran impatient fingers through his wet hair.

Libby watched, beguiled, as one damp curl fell over his broad forehead and a droplet ran down his sharply chiseled nose to fall on his umcompromisingly square chin.

Impatiently, the man shook his head, scattering water all over the hall's beautiful ivory damask wallpaper.

"Ask your bride-to-be!" Myrna flung an accusing hand toward Libby and stormed out of the apartment.

The man turned in the direction Myrna had pointed and frowned as he caught sight of Libby for the first time. Slowly his eyes wandered over her, touching on her tumbled hair, skimming over her small straight nose, lingering a second on her soft, full lips devoid of lipstick, before wandering downward.

Libby sucked in her breath and had to force herself not to back up in instinctive retreat. But she couldn't stop her body's involuntary reaction to his inspection. Her breasts swelled under his knowing gaze, their tips hardening, a fact that was impossible to hide.

Libby raised her chin and stared back at him, refusing to be ruled by her body's unexpected response to him.

Grim amusement quirked the corner of his well-shaped mouth as he registered her involuntary reaction. His interest slipped lower, dwelling on the slight swell of her abdomen before it came to rest in rapt absorption on the juncture of her thighs.

Libby felt the muscles of her stomach flutter in response and a shiver of uncertainty cooled her anger, allowing the rational part of her mind to gain ascendency. This man was not at all in the normal mode of her father's protégés. No one would call him shy or introverted. He positively oozed experience and only an idiot would doubt his self-confidence.

Apprehensively Libby faced him, refusing to allow her eyes to stray down the bare length of his magnificent body.

"You—" She stopped, cleared her throat and doggedly continued, "you are Joseph Landowski, aren't you?"

"Yes." The word was clipped. "And who the hell are you?"

Libby ignored the question, a wave of absolute fury washing over her. This was even worse than she'd originally thought. To have been exposed to the ridicule of all her friends by a shy young man who didn't know the social customs of the country was bad enough, but to be the victim of a practical joke was infinitely worse.

"I'll tell you who I am, you . . . you . . ." Libby waved the contract in his face.

"Let me see that." He grabbed the contract, not seeming to notice when his towel slipped.

Libby's eyes widened and, horrified at the direction her thoughts were taking, she hastily fixed her attention on a spot above his left shoulder.

"Sorry." Joe refastened his towel. "I'm not at my best this time of night."

If that wasn't his best, she'd like to see what was; the irreverent observation wouldn't be suppressed.

"Then I suggest you get dressed." Libby's voice sounded impossibly prim, but she didn't care. Over six feet of well-muscled, almost nude masculinity was simply too distracting.

"Hmm? Oh, sure," Joe stopped reading long enough to mutter. "Have a seat, I'll be right back, Liberty Joy Michalowski?" He arched a questioning blond eyebrow at her.

"Yes, I'm Libby Michalowski and you can bet your bottom dollar I'll stay. I've a lot to say on the subject of practical jokers."

"No doubt," Joe said sourly. "Everyone seems to have a lot to say tonight and none of it good." He shot a rueful glance at the door through which Myrna had left.

"Well, if you wouldn't . . ." Libby began hotly, but he ignored her as he stalked off toward the bedrooms and Libby closed her mouth with a snap. He'd be back and then she'd tell him exactly what she thought of what he'd done. She sank down on the edge of the cream linen sofa and waited.

2

LIBBY DIDN'T HAVE LONG TO WAIT. He was back in no more than five minutes, a pair of beige slacks covering his long legs and a navy knit shirt stretched over his broad chest.

She shot to her feet as he approached. As big as Joseph Landowski was, he tended to dwarf her own slight, five-eight frame and she didn't want to feel physically dominated by him. As most people would, Libby surmised shrewdly. His very size was intimidating. But he wasn't going to intimidate her. She was the one with the grievance. A very legitimate grievance. The faint echo of the appellation "cowgirl" drifted through her mind, and she opened her mouth to blast him.

"Stop right there." Joe held up one large hand. "Before you give vent to all the choice epithets no doubt hovering on your tongue, allow me to disclaim all knowledge of this document."

"You are Joseph Landowski, aren't you?

"Yes, I'm Joe Landowski." He sank down into a brown leather Eames lounger and propped his large, bare feet on the matching ottoman.

"And you live at 4 East Seventy-second Street, apartment 11-D, don't you?" Libby persisted.

"Right again." Joe nodded his blond head.

"And you expect me to believe that your name appeared on this iniquitous document by coincidence?" Libby eyed him with disgust.

"No." He sighed. "By my father."

"Your father?"

"I don't know how or when, but I sure know why," he admitted.

"So tell me, I don't."

"Because he wants to see me married and busily siring a pack of grandkids," he said shortly. "And he obviously feels that you'd make an acceptable wife."

"But I've never met your father," she protested. "Unless..." She remembered the old man who'd delivered the contract. "Is he in his early seventies, about five-five and stick thin? With a penchant for playacting?" She recalled his ridiculous period costume.

"No." Joe frowned. "The age is right, but my father's six-four and slightly overweight. Who were you thinking of?"

"The man who delivered that." Libby gestured to the contract Joe was still holding.

"Probably someone he hired."

"Maybe," she said dubiously, remembering the man's inbred dignity. He hadn't struck her as anyone's hireling.

"But how the contract was delivered isn't important," he began.

"That's what you think!" she snapped. "You'd feel differently if it had been handed to you in the middle of a party you were giving."

"Probably." His brilliant blue eyes gleamed with suppressed laughter and his lips twitched.

"It isn't funny! I'll probably still be hearing about this when I'm ninety."

"Perhaps," Joe conceded, "but at the moment I'm more interested in this." He stabbed the document with one large forefinger. "And why you were chosen to be the recipient."

"Same answer." Libby grimaced. "You aren't the only one with a manipulative father. I don't have the slightest doubt that he engineered the whole thing."

"Does this kind of thing all the time, does he?"

"Not this bad." She shuddered. "This time he's really surpassed himself. Normally his matchmaking is confined to introducing me to every eligible male he can lay his hands on. And some not so eligible ones," she added darkly, remembering a couple of borderline specimens he'd dredged up over the years.

"I know exactly what you mean," he commiserated. "My father's the same way." It's gotten so bad recently that I check with his housekeeper to see who else has been invited before I accept any of his dinner invitations. I keep telling him that I'm perfectly capable of choosing my own wife."

Libby's eyes flew to the door. "If Myrna was a sample of your girlfriends, then I should think so. She was stunning." Libby forced herself to give an honest opinion.

"To look at," he agreed absently as he read the contract, "but she's not the kind of woman one marries."

"Oh?" She frowned slightly, wondering what kind of woman one did marry, but before she could ask, Joe broke into laughter.

"Did you read the last paragraph of the second page?" He demanded.

"No, the first page was enough to raise my blood pressure fifty points."

"It says—" he chuckled "—that you agree to present me with six kids."

"Six!" She gasped.

"You probably wouldn't have time anyway," he said with a spurious sympathy that set her teeth on edge. "How old are you?"

"Thirty!" She was outraged at what she saw as a slur on her age. "And I would choose not to have six children for intellectual reasons, not chronological ones."

"Thirty?" He eyed her shapeless sweatshirt speculatively. "Perhaps it's your clothes," he added obscurely.

"And how old are you, Joseph Landowski?" Libby snapped.

"Thirty-six" He readily supplied the information. "But age in the father is irrelevant. Confucius's father was in in his seventies when he sired him."

"Since I don't aspire to have a son who wanders around the countryside spouting aphorisms, that's irrelevant."

"What do you want your sons to do?"

"Something useful," Libby shot back.

"What do you do?"

"I teach."

"What grade?"

"Mostly postgraduate math." She took a great deal of satisfaction out of wiping the condescending expression off his face. Patronizing male chauvinist, she thought angrily. What grade do you teach indeed!

"Abelian groups are my specialty," she threw in for good measure.

"Are they? Well, as they say, there's no accounting for taste. I've . . ." He paused thoughtfully. "Would you be related to Michalowski, the physicist?"

"Daughter," Libby said succinctly. "Only child, come to that. Dad retired in January, which simply gives him all the more time to think up devious new ways to find me a husband." She gestured toward the contract.

"It does make one wonder where he discovered my father. A theoretical physicist and a retired garment maker are an unlikely pair of conspirators."

"Trio," Libby corrected him. "Remember the man who delivered it."

"A triumverate of conspirators. That sounds more in keeping with what happened anyway. Rather like a bad Shakespearean comedy. But where they met is irrelevant. What is relevant is what we intend to do about the situation."

"What can we do, short of murdering them?" She sighed. "I've talked until I'm blue in the face and he just tells me not to be nervous."

"What about appealing to your mother?"

"Hopeless. My mother thinks that the pinnacle of success for every woman is reached when she manages to drag some hapless man to the altar. Everything after that is strictly anticlimactic."

"Not an advocate of women's lib, I take it?" He laughed.

"She seems to be supremely happy living through my father, and if that's what she wants, fine. I just wish she'd allow me to find happiness in my own way."

"I take it she nags?"

"Oh, no." She shook her head. "Mama's much too subtle for that. She does things like knit baby sweaters. I still remember when I received my Ph.D. She cried for three days solid."

"She must have been very proud of you."

"No, it wasn't that. She was afraid that I'd never catch a husband with the added handicap of a doctorate."

"Oh?" He blinked.

"Mmm." She nodded emphatically. "Men tend to shy away from women who are better educated than they are."

"Are you against marriage, per se?"

"No, and neither am I against children, although having six is ludicrous in this day and age. It's just that I'm not mentally constructed to bury myself in the suburbs. I'd go mad. I need the stimulation of my teaching, and the men I've dated seemed to think that a wife's place is in the home."

"Someone's got to take care of the kids."

"But why the wife? Why is it always the wife who's expected to put her career on hold and sit home with the kids?" she demanded.

"Because the wife earns less than the man."

"Not always. How much do you make a year?"

"After taxes?"

"Yes, your disposable annual income."

"Approximately two hundred thousand," he replied blandly.

"House-sitting!" Libby stared at him in dumbfounded amazement.

"House-sitting? What are you talking about?"

"You mean you own this place?"

"Of course I... Oh..." Comprehension dawned. "You thought I was simply keeping an eye on it?"

"Uh-huh." She nodded, feeling like an idiot. "At first I thought you were one of those shy, retiring political refugees my father occasionally helps get established. But one look at you and the exotic Myrna and I jettisoned that idea."

"But not the rest," he said, laughing, and Libby took exception to the sound. Where on earth had her father found Joe's parent? He'd certainly outdone himself this time.

"Anyway..." She doggedly returned to the original conversation. "Simply because you make more money..."

"A lot more money," he interjected, but she ignored him.

"Doesn't mean that you should automatically be the one to continue working."

"There are other considerations." His eyes fastened on the slight swell of her breasts. "Somehow I can't see me nursing a baby, can you?" he asked sardonically.

Libby's eyes flew to his broad chest, picturing the thick pelt of hair that covered it as well as the two flat masculine nipples nestled there. A warmth flooded her at the thought. A warmth that she determinedly ignored. Joe was a very attractive man, but she refused to allow herself to fall victim to that charm. She had enough to contend with without adding unwanted sexual attraction to the list.

"Speaking of nourishment, I'm starved." He stood up. "Myrna and I were about to have a snack when I accidentally doused myself with the champagne I was opening."

"Yes, Myrna." Libby winced. "I'm sorry about that. If you'll give me her address, I'll go and explain to her."

"Explain what?" Joe said dryly. "The fact that we have a couple of nuts for fathers? Thanks just the same, but I'd prefer to keep that particular piece of information under wraps. Besides, it was time Myrna went anyway. Come on, let's go raid the refrigerator."

"Okay." She followed him, a little chilled by the way he had dismissed Myrna with about as much feeling as he might dispose of yesterday's paper. But it wasn't any of her business, she told herself. Nothing about Joseph Landowski was. Their only point of contact was their fathers' conspiracy.

"Have a seat." He nodded toward the cane stool beside the breakfast bar.

Libby climbed onto it, glancing around the kitchen curiously. It certainly didn't look like the kitchen of a bachelor establishment. She studied the arrangement of well-worn copper pans hanging from a wrought-iron rack above the workmanlike center island.

"Nice." She accepted the glass of champagne he handed her. "Big, too."

"It has to be." He placed bagels, cream cheese and lox in front of her. "In case you hadn't noticed, I'm rather large."

"You cook?" She diverted.

"Bake." Joe sat down beside her and Libby felt the skin on her right arm prickle into instant life as the heat from his body wafted over her.

Determinedly she split an onion bagel and began to slather it with cream cheese. She refused to even acknowledge the inexplicable attraction his body held for her. She'd always mistrusted instant physical attraction. It made no sense. Friendships, even those that ripened into something more intimate, took time to develop. But then she wasn't talking about friendship, she thought wryly. She was talking about sex and that was not the same thing at all.

"At one time," he continued, seemingly unaware of the effect he was having on her central nervous system, "I had plans to become one of the world's great pastry chefs."

"So what happened?" she asked absently, looking around for a napkin to wipe off the cream cheese she'd smeared on her finger.

"Allow me." Her hand was engulfed in his much larger one.

Libby shivered at the feel of his hard fingers closing over hers. It gave her a curiously unsettled feeling. A feeling of having been claimed.

Joe carried her hand to his mouth and to her surprise licked the spot of cream cheese off her thumb.

The slightly rough feel of his tongue moving over her soft skin registered in her mind, shortening her breath and flooding her body with heat. This would never do. Joseph Landowski wielded his masculinity like a weapon and what was worse, he seemed to do it instinctively. Cautiously she stole a glance at his profile only to find his gaze fixed on her, a smile of polite inquiry curving his firm lips.

"Okay?" he asked.

"A napkin would have sufficed." She pointedly withdrew her hand.

"Waste not, want not," he shot back, and while she wasn't certain exactly what he meant, she decided it was definitely better not to ask. The sooner the door was closed on any conversation with sexual overtones, the better.

"We were talking about your abortive career as a pastry chef," she reminded him.

"Pity." Joe sighed and turned his attention to his bagel. "At any rate, when my brother decided not to follow Dad into the business that only left me."

"You've got a brother! Why doesn't your father work on him?"

"Because Stan became a priest. He's a bishop now."

"That would slow even my father down." She chuckled.

"Mmm—" he began to pile lox on his bagel "—it saved Stan, but it sure increased the pressure on me."

"It's a shame you had to give up your baking, though."

"Best thing that ever happened to me," he unexpectedly responded. "I'd have been bored stiff within a month stuck in some restaurant's kitchen. Now business is something else again. It's absolutely exhilarating pitting your wits against banks, restrictive trade laws, world economic conditions, recalcitrant labor and the fickleness of the American buying public."

"Not to me it isn't," Libby disagreed.

"To each his own." Joe reached for the coffeepot and poured them each a steaming cup. "To me those math classes of yours sound deadly dull."

"Dull!" Her mouth dropped open at his choice of words.

"Absolutely." He passed her the sugar and cream, which she ignored. "Math always follows certain rules, doesn't it?"

"Yes." Libby replied, nodding.

"So where's the excitement? If you do A, then B will follow ad nauseum. Whereas in business, nothing is an absolute. The whole economy is in a constant state of flux."

"Sounds rather disorganized to me!" she snapped, annoyed at his dismissal of the whole field of math as dull.

"Exhilarating," he corrected her. "But don't let it worry you. Everyone's different. I imagine you like being staid." His eyes danced with laughter, but she was too shocked at being labeled staid to notice.

"Simply because I happen to like things to follow a predictable sequence does not mean that I am staid!"

"If you say so," Joe replied blandly, "but that's all beside the point. The question facing us is what we are going to do to stop all this parental interference. Ever since my father retired last year, it's become impossible."

"Hasn't it though," she agreed. "It used to be that Dad only thought about my blissfully singular state in his spare time, which, thankfully, he didn't have that much of. But now—" she shrugged in resignation "—now I seem to be his one and only project."

"It's obvious that something is going to have to be done." He thoughtfully munched on his gargantuan sandwich.

"I know!" She brightened as an idea occurred to her. She grabbed his forearm in excitement, then quickly removed her hand when the muscles beneath her fingers flexed.

"You can pretend to court me and I'll tell my father that you're the greatest thing since sliced bread. I'll go off into rhapsodies about you every time I see him. No really," she insisted at his skeptical look. "I'll spread it on with a trowel."

"So how's that going to help?"

"That won't, but when you suddenly drop me, it will. I can carry on as if my whole life had been shattered. Maybe I could even go into a decline," she mused.

Joe shook his head. "Declines are for petite, ultrafeminine blondes."

"I may not be some pint-size blonde," Libby protested, strangely hurt at his observation, "but I'm certainly feminine enough."

"I'll have to take your word for it." He continued to munch contentedly on his bagel. "In that outfit you're wearing I can't tell. Women should wear skirts unless they're grossly overweight." He glanced down at her slim denim-clad legs, measuring her trim shape. "And you certainly aren't overweight."

"We've wandered rather far from the point," she reminded him. "We were discussing ways to slow down our respective fathers."

"Your idea wouldn't work." He shook his head again.

"Sure it would."

"For you, maybe, but what about me? I'd never hear the end of it if I were to behave in such a cavalier fashion as to break the heart of some poor girl."

"Woman," Libby muttered.

"And not just any girl." He warmed to his theme. "But a good Polish girl. The whole family would get into the act." He shuddered melodramatically.

"I guess." She sighed, knowing he was right. She picked up her coffee and began to sip it, then glanced down at it in surprise. "This is pretty good." She always gave credit where credit was due. "In fact it's better than I can make."

"I don't doubt there's lots of things I can do better than you can." Joe accepted her compliment with a complacency that set her teeth on edge, but she refused to rise to his teasing. Joe Landowski was a thoroughly exasperating man with no appreciation of the finer things of life, she thought, remembering his attitude toward her beloved math.

She sipped her coffee, strangely reluctant to be finished. She was inexplicably drawn to this man, despite the fact that he wasn't at all the type who normally appealed to her. He was too big, too assertive, too sexy and most especially too chauvinistic, she decided, recalling his dismissal of the unfortunate Myrna.

"Another bagel?" He pushed the bag toward her.

"No, thanks." Libby yawned. "It's time I was going."

"Not until we've figured out what we're going to do about this ridiculous situation."

"I thought we'd already decided that there was nothing we could do. At least nothing legal or moral." She grimaced.

"No." He refilled their empty coffee cups. "What we decided was that we couldn't stop them."

"That's what I said!"

"Not at all. There's a lot of ground between doing nothing and stopping them. That's what comes of being a mathematician. You're not used to looking at a problem from different angles. You're so used to going from point A to point C by way of B that it never occurs to you that you can also go to D and back up."

"This whole conversation sounds like it was backed into! Would you mind getting to the point, providing there is one."

"Certainly," he obliged. "Would you agree that our basic problem at present is not so much the fact that our fathers are trying to marry us off, but that now they've retired they have a lot more free time to devote to the project?"

"Yes," she concurred. "It's the stepped-up activity that's starting to get to me, not the basic problem. Over the years I've become pretty adept at avoiding my father's candidates."

"I know what you mean. At any rate, we need to find something to occupy their minds. And quickly, before they come up with something to top this." He waved toward the contract sitting on the counter.

"Impossible!" She shuddered. "Last night was an all-time high. Or low, depending on your point of view."

"What odds will you give me?" Joe laughed.

"None." Libby sighed. "But that also describes the ideas I have. I've tried talking, arguing, getting mad. Nothing works. Dad continues to plot."

"Then since we aren't going to stop them, the thing to do is to divert them."

"How?"

"By pretending to go along with this." He nudged the contract with a finger.

"You mean marry?" she gasped. "That's your creative solution?" A totally irrational spark of feeling flared to life only to be extinguished by his vehement denial.

"Of course not! When I marry it'll be because I decide it's time to, not because my father wants me to."

"So exactly what is your bright idea?"

"That we negotiate the contract." He leaned toward her and the faint odor of very expensive, masculine cologne drifted into her nostrils, coloring her feelings for a second. "Libby, quit playing the absentminded professor and pay attention."

His astringent voice broke into her thoughts and she hastily gathered her wits. What on earth was the matter with her? Going off into a daydream over the scent of a man's cologne. This fiasco must have affected her more deeply than she'd realized.

"I wasn't daydreaming," she lied. "I was thinking."

"To no avail from what I've seen."

"What good is negotiating the contract going to do if we have no intention of honoring it?" she demanded.

"It'll buy us time," he explained patiently. "We can keep them so busy mediating demands and counterdemands that they won't have any time to think up new methods to embarrass us."

"You think so?" She sounded skeptical.

"I know so. Consider it. Tonight you were given a preliminary contract."

She nodded.

"Supposing tomorrow we hammer out a counterproposal and you give it to your father. He's then going to have to get a hold of the other two members of his unholy alliance, set up a meeting and spend a great deal of time discussing the contract. And if I know them, offering alternate suggestions. They'll have to have it retyped and then deliver it to me this time. It'll take them days to get that far and once I have it, we can start the whole process over again."

"Hmm." She chewed her lower lip as she considered his idea. It wasn't foolproof, but it did have a lot to recommend it. It was certainly better than any idea she could come up with, she admitted fairly. "It might work."

"Of course it will," he insisted. "We ought to be able to keep them busy the better part of the summer."

"It's worth a try."

"It's a deal." Joe held out one large hand and Libby reluctantly put her own in it. His warm fingers closed over hers, and once again she felt that undeniable tug of attraction.

"It's settled then." She nodded. "We'll pretend to negotiate the contract."

"No."

"No?" Libby blinked in confusion, her tired mind not operating at its normal level of efficiency. "But you said—"

"I meant no we can't go into this project thinking in terms of pretense or we'll get exactly nowhere. Basically, what we're doing is acting, and the essence of acting is immersing yourself in the role."

"What would you suggest?" she asked dryly. "That I go over to the UN tomorrow and listen to them frustrate each other?"

"Not a bad idea since we're planning on thwarting our fathers." Joe grinned. "But I don't think you'd better. You're intractable enough without picking up any bad habits from that group."

"Intractable . . ." she sputtered, but he ignored her.

"What we should do is to negotiate as if this were real."

"You mean as if we might get stuck with the results?" she replied waspishly.

"Precisely." He beamed at her as if pleased by her quick understanding. "We'll both treat the negotiations as real and binding. That'll add a degree of authenticity that'll drive our fathers crazy."

"A short ride, the way things are going."

"And it'll be good practice in case you ever do manage to find a man."

"I'm not looking!" she snapped. His constant harping on her supposed inability to marry was beginning to grate. "And when I do choose a mate, a contract won't be necessary because I intend to marry someone exactly like me."

"I don't want someone like me." His eyes gleamed with mirth. "I intend to marry a member of the opposite sex."

Libby clamped her teeth together and refused to answer. Some forms of provocation were best ignored. Especially at three in the morning.

3

THE MUTED BUZZ of the phone on the bedside table drilled into Libby's deep sleep, shattering her slumber.

Groggily she rolled over, burrowing under her thick down pillow. It wasn't thick enough. The determined sound followed her, ricocheting through her mind and causing her stomach to lurch protestingly. She levered her head up, brushed the tangled strands of hair out of her face and peered blearily at the bright red numbers on her digital clock.

"Eight-thirty?" she muttered in protest. Who would be calling her at 8:30 on a Saturday morning? All her friends had been at her party last night and if they had any sense they'd still be asleep. Which was where she wished she was. When the ringing continued persistently, Libby grabbed the offending instrument.

"Hello!" she barked.

"Are you always this grumpy in the morning?" a deep male voice demanded.

"This isn't morning. It's the middle of the night." She ignored the unexpected frisson of pleasure that danced across her skin at the sound of Joe's voice.

"At eight-thirty on a gorgeous June morning?"

"I don't care what time it is. It doesn't become morning until I've had at least six hours of sleep. And I might remind you that it was almost four o'clock by the time you dropped me off."

"And I might remind you that showing up at my apartment at two in the morning was your bright idea, not mine."

"Details." She dismissed his words, beginning to wake up enough to wonder why he wasn't asleep himself. After all, he'd been up as late as she had. And, more importantly, why was he calling her? She would have thought that he'd have been very busy this morning placating the luscious Myrna. Apparently he'd meant what he'd said about it being time she went. A totally inexplicable sense of anticipation began to filter through her groggy mind.

"Why did you call? Other than to wake me up."

"To tell you to get out your swimsuit."

"What?" She frowned at the dust motes dancing in the sunlight pouring through her bedroom window.

"I thought you said you didn't want six kids."

Shaking her head in confusion, she said, "What I want is a conversation I can follow. You sound like a Philadelphia lawyer."

"And you sound like you've got an IQ of fifteen!"

"At least mine's measurable! Which is more than can be said for yours." She sniffed.

"With that tongue of yours it's no wonder you haven't managed to find a husband yet."

Libby gritted her teeth and refused to respond, a fact that seemed to disappoint him.

"Look," he said, "we need to begin negotiations, right?"

"Yup."

"And it's a beautiful day, right?"

"The weather is quite exceptional, but there seem to be a few disquieting tremors in the atmosphere."

"So you get your swimsuit, and I'll pick you up in half an hour. We'll spend the day at the beach negotiating the contract. Okay?" He managed to sound pathetically hopeful, a circumstance she instinctively mistrusted. Short though her acquaintance with Joe Landowski was, she was willing to bet that he was the type to grab what he wanted, not to sit back and wait for it to come to him. But it did sound like fun, she admitted. A leisurely day at the beach would be heavenly.

"Okay," Libby agreed, basking in his pleased murmur.

"I'll be over in half an hour."

"Half an hour! You just woke me up. At least you started the process. As late as I was getting to bed last night, it's going to take a minimum of a shower and a pot of coffee to restore me to some semblance of normalcy."

"Half an hour," he repeated, hanging up on her protests.

Of all the high-handed males! Who did he think he was that all he had to do was to dictate and she'd jump! For a second she considered refusing to go with him, but two things stopped her. She was curious to see if her uncharacteristic attraction to him last night had been borne of a combination of anger, embarrassment and the lateness of the hour or if there was more to it than that. Would he appear as overwhelmingly attractive in the clear light of day?

And, more importantly, the problem of her father's interference still remained. She winced as she remembered the infamous contract. Something had to be done and short of patricide, Joe's was the only viable idea she could think of. With a bit of luck, they might manage to tie the conspirators up for the whole summer. And by fall perhaps their fathers would have found some other interests to help fill all the free time that retirement had given them. It was certainly worth a try. Libby reluctantly got out of bed and dragged her protesting body into the bathroom.

Twenty minutes later she had finished her third cup of coffee and was beginning to feel more like her normal self. She was debating having yet another cup when the doorbell rang. Her eyes flew to the clock on the kitchen wall. He was ten minutes early. Inexplicably her heart began to race, and she ran suddenly damp palms down the legs of her jeans. She slid off the breakfast stool and slowly walked to the door, telling herself not to be ridiculous. He was simply a man and a rather aggravating one at that.

She peered through the peephole, her heartbeat returning to normal as she saw Jessie. Curious about what had brought her friend over so early, Libby unchained the door and swung it open.

"I remembered!" Jessie blurted out.

"Good for you!" Libby grinned at her friend's excitement. "Would you like a cup of coffee while you regale me with what you've dredged out of your memory?"

"Dredged is right." Jessie yawned as she followed Libby out to the kitchen. "I couldn't get to sleep last night for trying to remember where I'd seen that old man. And finally it came to me while I was reading this morning's paper."

She accepted the steaming cup of coffee that Libby handed her. "Once I remembered, I knew I had to catch you before you went looking for this Landowski character."

"Why?" Libby poured herself a fourth cup and leaned back against the sink as she sipped it. "Let me guess. You saw him in court on a murder rap instead of vagrancy?"

"Worse." Jessie sighed. "Do you know who that old man was?"

"No, and at the rate you're going I never will."

"His Honor, Casimir Blinkle!"

"His what?"

"Honor," Jessie said impatiently, obviously disappointed by Libby's lack of reaction. "In legal circles he's considered to be one of the best Supreme Court justices New York State ever had."

"Retired, I take it," Libby said thoughtfully.

"How did you know?"

"An educated guess."

"So you must see, Libby, this puts a whole new light on that contract. You can't just storm over to this Landowski's apartment until we find out where Judge Blinkle fits into things. It's possible Landowski is his protégé and not your father's."

"Good advice, but a little late." Libby grimaced.

"A little late? You mean you've already been?" Jessie looked at her in horror.

"Last night," Libby admitted. "After everyone left. I kept thinking about that contract and the more I thought about it, the madder I got. So at two o'clock I stormed over to give him a piece of my mind."

"And?" Jessie demanded.

"He wasn't at all what I expected."

"No small, shy retiring refugee?"

"He'd make two small men and nothing less than divine intervention could turn him into retiring."

"Oh?" Jessie's eyes lit up with interest. "Do tell."

"Restrain your curiosity. Suffice it to say that he was as appalled by the document as I was. Apparently I'm not the only one with a manipulative father."

"Was he upset by your arrival?"

"It could have been worse." *But I'm not sure how*, she thought.

"So now what?" Jessie asked.

"He's coming over in a few minutes and we're going to discuss what to do."

"Good, I'll help."

"You can help by getting lost. We're doing our discussing at the beach."

"Oh?" The drawn-out syllable held a wealth of innuendo.

"Joe has an idea."

"I'll just bet he does," Jessie said significantly. "It probably occurred to him the minute he laid eyes on you."

"No," Libby denied, refusing to admit even to herself the pique she felt at the admission. "If you could have seen the gorgeous redhead he was entertaining when I barged in last night . . ."

"You're more than a match for any redhead," Jessie said loyally.

"Marilyn Monroe couldn't have competed with this lady."

"That settles it. I'm not leaving until I get a peek at this Landowski character." Jessie settled herself more firmly on the seat. "And don't you try and talk me out of it. I don't like the sound of any of this. Can I have a piece of that cake?" she asked, changing the subject.

"Sure." Libby reached for a plate and cut her a piece. "I think I'll wrap it to take with me. Once I wake up I'm going to be hungry."

"Which beach are you going to?"

"I don't know. He didn't say, but—" Libby broke off as the doorbell rang.

"Ah-hah! The shy, retiring protégé."

"Come and meet him," she invited unnecessarily, since Jessie was hard on her heels. She swung open her front door, wincing as Jessie's astounded gasp filled the air.

Although she really didn't blame her friend, Libby decided. Her tired mind hadn't been exaggerating his physical presence last night; Joe Landowski was every bit as impressive in the full light of day. Her eyes were drawn to his silver belt buckle, which gleamed in the dim light of the hallway, then down over his flat belly to linger on the worn denim that hugged his muscular thighs.

"You weren't kidding when you said you were still asleep, were you?" Laughter threaded his warm voice, shattering her absorption.

Feeling like a gauche teenager, she invited him in and turned to introduce him to the stunned-looking Jessie.

"Jessie." She unobtrusively kicked her. "This is Joe Landowski. Joe, Jessie Anders."

"I'm pleased to meet you, Joe." Jessie didn't sound any too certain of the fact. "I was just leaving."

"It was a pleasure to have made your acquaintance." He gave her a courtly bow that somehow seemed natural.

"Goodbye. I'll see you later, Libby."

Not sure if that was a promise or a threat, she murmured, "Anytime," and closed the door behind Jessie. She motioned Joe into her living room. "If you want to sit down, I won't be but a moment. I just have to get my things."

"I don't mind waiting if you want to put on a skirt."

"I like jeans and, besides, you're wearing them."

"In case you haven't noticed, I'm a man."

"I've noticed a whole lot more than merely your gender," Libby said ominously. "Just sit down, I'll be right back."

She hurried into the kitchen, stuffed the wrapped pieces of cake into her beach bag, which already contained her swim wear and the contract, and sped back into the living room.

"Which beach are we going to?" she asked.

"Mine," he replied, leaving her to wonder which of the area's many beaches he considered his.

It wasn't until they were actually pulling into a private driveway somewhere on the south side of Long Island that she realized that when he'd said 'mine,' he'd meant exactly that. She glanced around with interest. About five hundred yards to the right was a soaring glass-and-cedar home, and to their extreme left was a huge gabled mansion, which could have come straight out of *The Great Gatsby*.

"Quite a neighborhood." She studied the thick shrubbery, which effectively blocked his house from view.

"Uh-huh." He unfastened his seat belt, released hers and then leaned across her to push open the car door.

Libby shrank back in her seat as the hard bar of his forearm brushed against her breasts. Her breath caught in her lungs at the unexpected contact, and she could feel her soft curves swelling under the slight pressure. An irrational urge to lean forward into his tanned flesh shook her, and she bit her lip to break the spell that seemed to have effortlessly ensnarled her unwary senses.

What's the matter with you, she demanded of her stunned mind. She hadn't had a purely physical reaction of such intensity since she'd been an impressionable teenager who'd judged a man solely on his physical attributes. Over the years she'd learned discernment. She'd discovered that what a man looked like on the outside wasn't necessarily synonymous with what he was like on the inside. Now she was mature enough to judge men by their actions, not their faces.

So why was she coming unglued at Joe's casual touch? The unanswerable question surfaced. Fortunately, since an acceptable answer evaded her, he removed his arm and, taking a deep breath to still her skittering senses, Libby climbed out of the car.

"There is a house down there, isn't there?" she asked, voicing her suspicions aloud.

"Uh-huh." He transferred her beach bag to his left hand and lightly grasped her arm in his right. "Although not on the scale of the neighbor's." He nodded toward the rambling mansion. "That monstrosity is simply too big to be practical."

"You surprise me," she said dryly. "Considering what you've already said, I'd have expected you to try to fill it with kids."

"An intriguing thought." His eyes gleamed for a brief moment and Libby's stomach flip-flopped. "But one must exercise some self-control."

"I'll believe that when I see it." She cautiously made her way over the deeply rutted path meandering through the dense undergrowth. "As a point of interest, why don't you clean all this out and plant some grass?" she asked. "You ought to be able to find a variety that'll grow this close to the ocean."

"Maybe, but if I did, then I'd have to mow it and since the whole purpose of this place is to relax . . ."

"It is very nice," she said in sincere appreciation as they finally emerged from the underbrush to see a split-level house built of a silvered wood nestled into the hillside.

"I like it. Although I don't get to spend as much time here as I'd like." Joe unlocked the gleaming black enameled door, swung it open and motioned her inside.

"You're lucky to have found it." She glanced curiously around the interior. The entire front of the house was one room that held an assortment of furniture that seemed gleaned from garage sales. Directly in front of her were two half flights of stairs. One led up to the bedrooms and the second down to the kitchen and dining area.

"Actually, I didn't find it," he admitted. "My father did. He bought it when he retired, as a summer getaway for his grandchildren."

"A gentle hint, I take it." She laughed.

"Gentle nothing," Joe snorted. "Let me show you the bedrooms." He led the way up the half flight of stairs to the third level and flung open one of the three doors fronting the hallway.

Libby peeked in, blinked and looked again. Everything in the room was in unrelieved blue, including the three sets of painted bunk beds!

"In case all six of those kids he put in the contract turn out to be boys."

"It would serve him right if they were girls. Then all this blue would be wasted."

"My father is nothing if not adaptable. Next door is an identical setup in pink."

"It makes my mother and her knitting baby sweaters look like small potatoes."

Joe chuckled at her rueful expression. "Why don't you change in here? I'll meet you downstairs in five minutes." He handed her her bag.

"Five minutes," she agreed.

When the blue door closed behind Joe, Libby quickly stripped off her jeans and cotton top and pulled on her swimsuit. She eyed herself dispassionately in the room's one mirror, suddenly uncertain of her choice. A fact that annoyed her greatly. She was a mature adult who knew what looked good. So what was it about Joe that had her suddenly doubting the sleek black Lycra? She had always subscribed to the theory that a one-piece suit, cut deeply enough to hint at her shape, was more seductive than a micro bikini that left nothing to the imagination. And she'd never doubted it until now.

Libby frowned thoughtfully at her slight curves exposed by the plunging neckline. She was too small to really do justice to the suit, she admitted honestly. But at least the rest of her fitted in with society's concept of a sexy, desirable woman. She viewed her flat stomach, trim hips and long slender legs with satisfaction.

But what difference did her figure make? She grimaced. She was only here to negotiate the contract. Vowing to behave exactly like the calm, competent professional that she knew herself to be, she picked up her towel and went in search of Joe.

She found him standing in front of the kitchen's sliding glass doors staring out at the ocean. Libby paused in the doorway as her eyes willfully traced the lines of his powerful body with something akin to hunger. He raised a hand to run long fingers through his thick blond hair, and she watched in fascination as the muscles in his back rippled. Her eyes compulsively followed the straight line of his spine down to where it disappeared into his brief, black racing trunks. Her eyes widened and her breathing developed an uneven cadence as she studied the way the stretchy material hugged the lean curves of his buttocks. She blinked to break the spell and purposefully strode into the room, her resolve to act normally wavering slightly as Joe turned and her eyes feasted on the broad expanse of chest in front of her.

He studied her through narrowed eyes, and Libby felt her toes curl into the flat outdoor carpeting that covered the kitchen floor as she wondered what he was thinking. The answer when it came was infuriating. He hadn't even seen her. He was studying her swimsuit!

"Bad choice," he pronounced.

"What is?"

"The swimsuit. With your coloring, you should be wearing clear, jewel tones, not black. Besides, that particular style squashes your breasts. You should either wear a thin cotton bikini that simply covers your natural shape or, if you insist on a one-piece, try one with a built-in bra."

"I beg your pardon!" Libby was outraged.

"No need to beg my pardon." He smiled at her. "I don't really care one way or the other, but if you're trying to attract a man, you ought to maximize what assets you have."

"I have lots of assets!"

"Of course you do," Joe soothed. "You're really in very good shape for thirty."

"You keep this up and I'll show you how good a shape I'm in," she fumed. "I'll give you a good swift kick in the shins."

"I don't know why you're so upset," he complained. "I was simply trying to give you the benefit of my experience."

"Keep your ill-gotten knowledge to yourself!"

"Gains."

"What?"

"The expression is ill-gotten gains. I'm not sure what goes with knowledge."

"Certainly not a sense of self-preservation or you'd shut up. If this is the way you behave with women, it's no wonder you're reduced to having to have your father find you a wife."

"People who live in glass houses shouldn't throw stones," he said piously.

"Or talk in maxims."

"*Mea culpa, mea culpa, mea maxima culpa.*" Joe smote his broad chest with one large fist, and Libby was unable to suppress a giggle at his patently false expression of repentance he wore.

"It certainly is your fault," she said, "and I'll return the favor and give you a piece of unsolicited advice. If you want our association to last even long enough to draft a counterproposal, then don't try to remake me into your idea of feminine beauty. I'm perfectly content the way I am."

"Ruts do tend to get comfortable, don't they?" he sympathized.

"You know, my friend, meeting you has shown me an unsuspected facet to my personality."

"Oh?" He peered uncertainly at her.

She nodded. "I've suddenly discovered that I'm capable of violence. I'm experiencing an overwhelming desire to throttle you."

"They say violence and passion are closely interwoven. You wouldn't care to try sublimation, would you?" he asked hopefully.

Even knowing that he was teasing, Libby was unable to entirely suppress the flood of desire that shook her. A fact that made her voice sharp.

"Tell me, is that the same 'they' who say that all women want to be mastered?"

"They don't?"

"Contrary to your chauvinistic imaginings, no. A normal woman wants a give-and-take relationship."

"But you aren't normal," he pointed out. "You're a thirty-year-old spinster with a Ph.D. in mathematics."

"You forgot my Phi Beta Kappa!" she snapped.

"What?"

"That's my mother's favorite refrain. You're an old maid of thirty with a Phi Beta Kappa in math. Of course, I can understand her viewpoint. She's sixty-seven, was born in Poland and never even graduated from high school. What's your excuse?"

"I don't need an excuse. I'm a man."

"Amen!"

"Dammit, Libby." Joe took a deep breath and her eyes widened as his narrow racing trunks slipped lower. "We can't get into a fight yet."

"You have one scheduled later on?"

With exaggerated patience, Joe replied, "What I mean is we came out here to iron out our differences."

"Iron nothing. It would take a sledgehammer to smooth them out."

"Nonetheless, we're going to give it our best shot. My father still annoys me more than you do."

Libby eyed him narrowly. "Thanks heaps, but I'm not sure that I can return the compliment."

"Don't worry about it. We'll work on it."

"That's what worries me," she mumbled as she walked through the sliding glass door Joe held open.

The crisp tang of the salt-laden air teased her nostrils and the pine-scented breeze dissipated her pique at his high-handedness. It was a glorious day. She breathed deeply, not noticing the way Joe's eyes narrowed as her slight breasts swelled. She was going to enjoy it, she assured herself, trying hard to believe it. It wasn't often that she was lucky enough to have the use of such a beautiful private beach, even if she did have to share it with a thoroughly exasperating man. She paused on the sandy ground about fifteen feet from the edge of the water and asked, "How about here?"

"Great." Joe spread out the large cotton blanket he was carrying and then plopped down on it.

Libby dug her toes into the gritty sand, and watched through lowered lashes as he rolled onto his back and rested his head on his folded arms. The sun turned the profusion of blond hair on his chest to liquid gold, and a fluttering sensation in her stomach began to erode her resolve to remain aloof.

"Let me guess," he said in resignation, "you don't like this spot after all?"

"It's fine." She got a firm grip on herself. If she weren't careful, he might realize the effect he was having on her nervous system and that would really convince him that she was a repressed spinster. Her pride demanded that she appear as insouciant as he.

She dropped down on the blanket, being careful not to touch him without being obvious about it. Putting on her dark glasses, she reached into her bag for her suntan lotion.

Joe shifted onto his side, and her leg prickled as his hair-roughened calf brushed against her soft flesh.

"A good idea," he observed. "The sun's pretty strong this time of year."

"Sure is," she blurted out, and hurriedly uncapped her lotion, fearing that he might offer to apply it for her. The very thought of his fingers stroking over her skin was enough to make her heart race.

She began slathering the thick cream on her exposed body with more haste than efficiency, but to her surprise and unacknowledged chagrin, he made no attempt to help. Instead he rolled over onto his stomach and closed his eyes. Refusing to even admit her disappointment, Libby finished coating herself and leaned back.

"Do me, would you?" he murmured sleepily.

"Do you?" she stalled. To refuse would brand her hopelessly unsophisticated, but to agree would mean exposing her already unsettled nerves to the feel of his taut flesh. She gnawed on her lower lip uncertainly. She was an adult, she reminded herself. Surely she could control her emotions for the length of time it would take to put suntan oil on him. At any rate she was hardly likely to lose control to the extent of flinging herself on him! The thought of her trying to take advantage of Joe was sufficient to make her giggle.

"It isn't funny," he complained. "I burn very easily and if I burn I'll be irritable and hard to get along with."

"You mean you could get worse?" Libby asked in mock astonishment. "I'm not sure that's possible."

"You have a sharp tongue."

"It seems to come naturally around you."

"Well, see if you can dredge up a little feminine compassion and rub some of that lotion on."

"There's hope for you yet if you're willing to admit that compassion's a feminine trait."

"So's insisting on the last word," Joe complained.

"Really?" She squeezed a stream of the chilly liquid over his back, smiling in satisfaction as he jerked in surprise. Setting down the bottle, Libby flexed her fingers, took a deep breath and began to massage it in. Her palms slid over his chamois-soft skin, and she could feel the strength of the muscles directly beneath it as he settled more comfortably into the sand.

Gamely she rubbed, working her way down his back. The heady scent of warm oil underlaid by the basic odor of Joe himself rose from his body to drift down her lungs and constrict her breathing. Her fingers soothed the lotion over the sensitive skin at the back of his neck and the ends of his hair pricked her skin, heightening her awareness of him. She gulped as she covered the tips of his ears, shivering as her hand accidentally scraped over the sandpaper texture of his jawline.

"There." Her voice sounded impossibly breathless even to her own ears. "All done."

"What about my legs?" he muttered drowsily.

"You can reach your own legs." She quashed her inclination to do it.

Joe rolled over on his side, propped himself up on one elbow and eyed her narrowly.

Libby forced herself to meet his gaze with what she hoped was a sophisticated smile. To her amazement, he reached out, grabbed her wrist and pulled her down on top of his chest.

For a brief second surprise held her still. Her nose was pressed into the crisp hair covering his chest, and her upper body was lying across his hard abdomen. She took a deep breath, which only served to further cloud the issue as the smell of sun-warmed skin flooded her consciousness. She gasped as his arms encircled her and pulled her upward along his length, raising her awareness of him to a fever pitch of excitement. Finding herself level with his face, she stared into his blue eyes, which seemed to darken with suppressed passion.

Libby ran the tip of her pink tongue over her dry lips as her concentration shifted to the firm line of his mouth. Her body burned where it touched him, and a tiny pulse in her neck hammered with frantic life. She was so caught up in the sensual spell he was weaving that she barely noticed when his large hand captured the nape of her neck and slowly pulled her downward. A second before their lips touched she tried to retreat, but it was too late. His mouth captured hers with a determination that brooked no denial. One muscular arm around her thigh held her tightly against him while the other held her head captive for him to explore her mouth at will.

She felt the tip of his tongue outline her lips and she instinctively opened her mouth, immediately realizing her mistake when his tongue plunged inside to explore the moist warmth. A tight coil of excitement began to build in her abdomen.

"No." She instinctively denied the torrent of sensation. To her amazement and secret dismay, Joe heeded her plea. With a casualness totally at variance to the cascading emotions tumbling through her veins, he calmly dumped her throbbing body back onto the blanket.

She put her arm across her eyes to shield her expression from his sharp gaze, took a deep steadying breath and demanded, "Why did you do that?"

"To clear the air," he replied calmly.

"To clear...?" Her voice rose in disbelief.

"Yes." He nodded emphatically. "You've been jumpy as a kitten ever since we arrived, expecting me to make a pass at you. Well, I made the pass, you survived the experience and now we can get down to the reason we came out here. The contract."

So that was how he'd interpreted her nervous awareness of his sexuality—as fear that he might make a pass. Libby wasn't sure if she preferred him to think she was some kind of shrinking violet who expected every man she came across to try to leap. But the truth—that she was leery of her unprecedented attraction to him—wasn't any better. Deciding that one choice was as bad as the other, Libby opted to ignore the whole mess.

"I've got the contract in my beach bag, but before we begin would you mind getting me something to drink?" She forced the words out past dry lips. "All this sunlight is making me very thirsty."

"Sure." Joe levered his body up with a lithe movement that spoke of superbly conditioned muscles and jogged back to the house.

Libby watched him go with relief. She desperately needed a few minutes to recover her poise.

BY THE TIME JOE HAD RETURNED with their drinks, Libby had regained her equilibrium and was able to accept the Coke he gave her with something approaching sangfroid.

"Better?" He eyed her indulgently as she gulped the icy liquid.

"Heavenly." She pressed the cold bottle against her sun-flushed cheek. "Absolutely heavenly."

"Good." He suddenly became brisk. "Where's that contract?"

Libby blinked. The hot sun on top of her lack of sleep was making her mental responses sluggish to say the least. She dug into her beach bag and pulled out the contract and a pen. "Here."

"Let me see that again." He stretched out and quickly re-read the two-page document.

"How did you manage to get a name like Liberty Joy?" he asked curiously.

"My parents spent the last two years of the Second World War in a prisoner-of-war camp and the next three at a displaced-persons camp waiting to emigrate. It's hardly any wonder that they placed a great deal of emphasis on liberty."

"No," he agreed. "I suppose we'd best take this proposal item by item."

"I'll take it item by item!" she said tartly. "It was delivered to me, remember? You'll get your turn when they give you the revised edition. You just write." She handed him the pen.

"Haven't you ever heard of the old saying, you catch more flies with honey than vinegar?"

"If that's a hint that I should trot out some dumb flattery in an attempt to get you to do the writing, forget it."

"It's not dumb."

"Oh, yes it is. Patronizing, too."

"Patronizing!" He arched one eyebrow.

"Yes, patronizing. Think about it. Instead of treating you like a rational adult and making a reasonable request, i.e., that you do the writing, I'd be treating you like an imbecile who can be manipulated by a bit of obvious flattery."

"You underestimate yourself." He grinned. "I'm sure that someone clever enough to get a Phi Beta Kappa key could manage to sound convincing."

"I've too much self-respect." She sniffed.

"What's the matter, Libby?" Joe gave her a falsely sympathetic smile that infuriated her. "Were you so busy being clever that you never learned how to play the game of courtship?"

"I know the rules of Russian roulette, too, but I've got better sense than to play it."

"Poor Libby." He gave her a pat on the head that made her feel like an erring puppy. "Tell you what. You can practice on me. What are friends for?"

"You aren't a friend," she said grimly. "You're a chance acquaintance and, at the rate you're going, you're much more likely to end up as an enemy than as a friend."

"Umm." Joe nodded his head solemnly. "Telling the truth does tend to make enemies."

Libby closed her eyes and counted to ten. Of all the aggravating men. No wonder he wasn't married. A woman would have to be desperate to take him on and she wasn't desperate. She'd never be that desperate.

"Go ahead and try. Don't be shy." The gleam in his bright blue eyes belied the sympathy in his voice. "I promise not to laugh at your efforts."

"You're going to be crying very shortly if you don't shut up!" she snapped. "Now, are you going to write or not?"

"Not." He shoved the paper toward her. "If you insist on acting like a man, you might as well do the work."

"I am acting like a mature adult," she stated even though the thought persisted that between the two of them their behavior didn't add up to one rational adult.

"Now then." She skimmed the first paragraph. "It starts off pretty straightforward. Just a recitation of names, ages and education. Hmm." She paused, rereading something she'd originally missed. "You don't have a college degree?"

"Nope, just two years of Harvard."

"What were you majoring in?"

"Economics."

"Why? I thought you wanted to be a chef?"

"My father wasn't very enamored of my chosen career, so we made a deal. I would get my degree and then, if I still wanted to be a chef, Dad would set me up in the pastry business. Unfortunately, right before my junior year Dad had a heart attack. It wasn't major but the doctor said he had to take it easy for a while. So I dropped out of college to help him with the company while he recuperated. I fully intended to go back to school the following year, but within two months I was hooked on running the business and I've been there ever since."

"Why don't you finish your degree? You could do it at night."

"Why?" Joe rolled over and studied her. "Why should I waste my evenings studying the theory when I spend my days putting it into practice? The trouble with you is that you're an educational snob."

"I am not!" she vehemently protested.

"Yes you are! You turn a simple piece of sheepskin into the pot of gold at the end of the rainbow. Or more precisely, into the ticket of entry into your social circle."

"That's not true." Libby was deeply shocked at his accusation. She prided herself on being liberal.

"Think a minute. How many of your friends don't have degrees?"

"Well . . . none . . ."

"Moreover, I'd be willing to bet that the vast majority of them have more than one."

"That's probably because I met most of them at the university," she replied, defending herself.

"If you say so." His voice conveyed a world of doubt, but Libby let the subject drop. His charge had shaken her and she wanted to examine it in private.

"Anyway, we've rather strayed from the point."

"You brought it up."

"This paragraph on the character of the bridegroom is a beaut!" She chewed on the end of her pencil.

"Oh, I don't know. I thought it rather accurate." He smirked.

"It reads like an advertisement for Prince Charming! Personally I prefer a low-key approach. I think I'll insert a specification for modesty." She made a notation in the margin.

"If you don't blow your own horn, no one else will."

Libby glanced up at him, her pencil poised over the page. "Then the world would be a much quieter place."

"I've heard of academics in their ivory towers, but aren't you carrying it to extremes?"

"I don't suppose the wording of this really matters, but—"

"Oh, yes it does." He cut her off. "And you're bright enough that I shouldn't have to tell you twice that we're negotiating this as if it were for real."

"Well, in that case, this has to go," she retorted.

"Which 'this' is that?" Joe slowly drained the last of his Coke.

"The paragraph on roles. It states that I will stay at home, run your house, entertain your guests and in exchange you will give me an allowance."

"Seems fair to me."

"I don't need an allowance. I'm a professional, well able to earn enough to take care of my own needs."

"You won't be working, if you're at home."

"Oh, yes I will. My work is very important to me. I'm not some junior typist killing time while waiting for some man to come along and marry me. I'm a highly skilled, highly trained educator. I love my work. There's no feeling on earth like the high you get when a student finally grasps what you're trying to teach him. And you expect me to give up all that to keep house?"

"It's a wife's job to run the house."

"Baloney!" Libby snorted. "You haven't got a wife, yet your apartment was in immaculate condition."

"I have a housekeeper," he admitted, "but it's really a wife's job."

"Why?" she demanded. "The idea is to have a clean, well-run home, right?"

"Yes, but . . ."

"Then why would you assume that the apartment's going to be any cleaner if the work is done as an act of love rather than as a job?"

"Wives are supposed to clean."

"Quit spouting those clichés and think, for heaven's sake!" Libby said in exasperation. "You want a clean home. Your housekeeper does a good job. So why would any rational person try to force a wife into a job she's ill equipped to do? Would you take your accountant and try to turn him into a computer programmer?"

"Of course not, but . . ."

"It's the same thing." Libby drove her point home. "You don't take one highly trained individual and substitute him for another. Not when there's an alternative."

"But if you aren't running the house, you'll be bored sitting around all day."

"You aren't listening. I won't because I won't be sitting around. I'll be teaching, as I've always done."

"No wife of mine is going to work outside the home!"

"But with you around, she's going to wind up doing plenty of work in it!"

"All right." Joe shrugged. "We'll compromise. I'll keep my housekeeper and you stay home."

"That's not a compromise," Libby said dryly. "That's total capitulation. However—" she made a notation in the margin "—I will accept your offer of a housekeeper."

"It figures," he said sourly. "You won't give, but you're perfectly willing to take."

"If I gave on that point, I'd be giving my sanity." She was unfazed by his charge. "But just to show that my heart's in the right place, I'll agree to be your hostess provided you give me twenty-four-hours' notice."

"Oh, I'd definitely say that your heart is in the right place." His gleaming eyes fastened on the soft swell of her left breast and Libby felt a physical reaction to the awareness.

"Right about here." He lazily reached out and placed his palm over the soft flesh. Her breath became suspended in her lungs, and the heart he was referring to began to beat a frenzied tattoo against her chest wall.

"Of course my heart's there." She tried not to let the effect he was having on her show in her voice. "I have all the standard anatomical parts."

"Oh?" His large forefinger lightly traced her skin along the bodice of her swimsuit.

A shiver chased over her skin and her spirit sank. Undoubtedly he was comparing her own slender curves with Myrna's lush femininity. She didn't have the slightest doubt which he preferred. But it made no difference, she told herself. Despite the strangeness of their relationship, they were simply business associates. Determinedly she reached for her Coke, using it as an excuse to move out of reach of his tantalizing fingers.

"About the next section . . ."

"But we haven't settled the last one yet," he protested.

"You'll get your chance when they return the contract to you." Libby read the next paragraph.

"This says that we'll live in a house on Long Island."

"Sounds reasonable."

"Only if you're a devotee of long train rides," she countered, "which I most definitely am not."

"But children need a big yard with room to roam."

"Children need their parents," she shot back. "If we were to live on Long Island, we'd be spending a minimum of two hours a day simply commuting. Time that could be spent with them, if we had an apartment in the city."

"Apartments are too crowded," he insisted. "Kids need lots of open space to play."

Libby shrugged. "So we take them to the park. Kids are a lot more adaptable than you're giving them credit for."

"If you stayed at home with them, only one parent would be commuting." Joe persisted.

"Listen to me very carefully," she enunciated clearly, deep annoyance in her tone. Momentarily she had suspended the knowledge that this was all a game. "I am not going to give up my job to be buried alive in suburbia."

"Negotiating with you is like negotiating with the Russians."

"Nonsense. I'm willing to admit that my apartment would be too small for a family. We'll use yours."

"How generous," he said sarcastically.

"Now then, most of the last page is concerned with the prospective family." Libby skimmed it.

"I don't doubt it." He sighed in resignation. "Dad has very definite views on the subject."

"Definite or not, six kids is out! One is plenty."

"One!" Joe was outraged. "One's not even worth getting started for. Besides, what happens if we get a girl?"

"Then we'll know we were doing something right if we're so blessed," she fumed.

"A man needs a son to pass his business on to."

"Girls have just as much business sense as boys!"

"Occasionally, but not normally. Look at you. You haven't the vaguest interest in big business."

"True," Libby conceded, completely unsympathetic to his viewpoint, although she was willing to admit that his wanting a son to follow in his footsteps was a relatively common attitude among men. Even among the men she knew.

"I want at least one son." Joe pressed his slight advantage.

"First of all, the sex of the baby is determined by the father and, secondly, we could wind up with a dozen daughters in the course of trying to get a son."

"I don't mind."

"Of course you don't. You're not the one who has to put up with morning sickness, dietary restriction and looking like a blimp for the better part of nine months," she said hotly. "Your total involvement takes a couple of seconds."

"You underestimate me." His mouth curved upward in a seductive smile. "It would take me hours to make love to you. Long, beguiling hours."

His velvety voice released a flood of images in Libby's mind, and she felt a warmth growing in her chest, expanding as her mind seemed to slip into a sensual fantasy with a will of its own. Resolutely she dragged her attention back to the problem at hand. "I don't care if you're promising an all-day orgy," she said tartly. "That doesn't begin to make up for the discomfort of being pregnant for nine months."

"How do you know unless you've tried it? I thought scientists were supposed to be big on firsthand experience. What are you writing?"

"That I want one child, but if it's a girl I agree to have a second."

"That's your idea of compromise?"

"It'll do for a start. Pass me my beach bag, would you please?"

Joe handed it to her and she dug out the wrapped pieces of cake.

"Want some?" She offered him one.

"Thanks, I'm starved." He unwrapped the cake and took a bite.

Libby watched in confusion as his look of expectation faded, to be replaced by on of pure horror. He swallowed and then glared down at the remainder.

"What the hell is it?"

"Cake, chocolate cake." She took a cautious bite of her own. It was fine. "It tastes all right to me."

"Where did you get this disaster?"

"I made it from a cake mix and the icing came out of a can."

"A can! No wonder it tastes like paraffin." Joe plucked the cake out of her hand and tossed the two pieces out onto the sand. "Let the gulls eat it. They don't know any better. That's a disgrace. I'll bet your mother never made a cake from a box."

About to say that since her mother didn't work she had lots of time to bake, Libby suddenly thought better of it. There was no sense bringing that up again.

"I'll show you how to bake a real cake."

"But I'm hungry now, not at some time in the nebulous future." She eyed the sand-covered cake regretfully.

"Okay." Joe unexpectedly stood up. "I'll buy you lunch. There's a place in town that serves the best lobster I've ever had."

"You're on." She took his hand and let him pull her up, feeling suddenly lighthearted. It was turning out to be a lovely day.

LIBBY SIGHED IN DISGUST as she flipped off the television. "You'd think there'd be something on to watch on a Wednesday night," she muttered. After all, eight o'clock was the beginning of prime time.

Grudgingly she picked up the stack of math papers waiting to be graded. She wasn't in the mood to do it. She felt restless. And had ever since she'd gone out to the island with Joe last weekend, she suddenly realized. The unwelcome knowledge sobered her, and she resolutely picked up her red pencil and turned to the first page.

She had worked halfway through an almost incomprehensible mathematical proof when the doorbell rang. Happily she dropped the garbled sheet of figures, grateful for any distraction.

She peered through the peephole and her heartbeat accelerated when she saw Joe. The rush of pleasure that washed over her was disquieting, but she ignored the feeling, releasing the chain and opening the door.

"Where's the kitchen?"

Libby automatically took one of the brown grocery sacks he handed her.

"And a good evening to you, too. Yes, it is a lovely night," she said tartly. "What's in here?" She poked her nose into the sack.

"Ingredients that belong in the kitchen. So if you'll just tell me where it is . . ."

"Through there." She pointed to the swinging door in the far wall. "This may seem like a silly question, but why are you bringing me groceries?" she asked, following him.

"This is a kitchen?" Joe looked down his nose at the tiny room.

"What's wrong with it?" She put her sack down on the single counter beside the sink.

"It's not big enough to swing a cat in."

"I don't have a cat," she replied absently as she watched him unload.

"Don't be facetious." He tenderly set a cake carrier down on the breakfast bar.

"I didn't bring up the cat, and I still don't know why you're standing in my kitchen insulting the amenities."

"I told you I would." Joe crumpled up the sack and tossed it in the general direction of the wastebasket. It landed on the floor, but she ignored the litter and tried to sort out his words.

"You mean you were serious when you threatened to teach me to bake a cake?"

"Promised." He opened her cabinets and peered inside. "I consider it my duty to teach you the error of your ways before you manage to poison someone with what you laughingly call a cake."

"What are you looking for?"

"Bowls. Ah." He reached up to the top shelf and took down a set of mixing bowls.

"This may come as a shock to you, friend, but I'm perfectly happy with my packaged mixes."

"You may be, but I'm not!" he said emphatically. "And, if our relationship is to prosper, you've got to learn at least some elementary baking."

Libby considered his words, wondering exactly what he meant. Was he referring to their partnership to thwart their fathers, or did he mean something else? Something more personal? For a moment a sense of elation filled her, then common sense intruded. Men who had girlfriends who looked like Myrna didn't lose their heads over thirty-year-old math professors.

"Besides," he continued when she didn't reply, "don't you know that the way to a man's heart is through his stomach? If you pay attention, you might learn enough to catch a husband."

"I told you that I'm not actively looking. Any man fool enough to marry a woman simply because she can cook is hardly much of a catch."

"What do you want in a man?" He gave her a curious look. "What does a highly educated, intellectual elitist look for in a husband?"

"I am not an intellectual elitist!" she yelled, "and if you suggest that I am one more time, I might descend to your level and resort to physical violence."

Joe paused unloading his sack. He studied the pugnacious tilt of her chin, then his gaze slid across her slender shoulders and came to rest on her slight arms.

Libby felt her skin tingle where his bright blue eyes seemed to touch her, which annoyed her intensely. She didn't want to be aware of a man who consistently insulted her. Unfortunately, her emotions seemed to have a will of their own.

"You couldn't physically intimidate a little old man, let alone me."

"Yeah?" she taunted. "And what's so special about you?"

He carefully placed a carton of eggs on the counter and walked over to her, stopping a scant inch away. That close, his height and the breadth of his shoulders were truly impressive. She eyed his bulging left bicep warily, but refused to retreat.

"I'm bigger than you are," he observed mildly. "Lots bigger."

"The bigger they are, the harder they fall," she muttered, unnerved by his closeness. The warmth of his big body enveloped her, heating her skin and bringing it to tingling life. The sharp tang of his after-shave infiltrated her senses and muddled her thought processes.

"You've been reading too many fairy tales." Joe suddenly reached out and, catching her off balance, pulled her to him.

Her small nose was crushed against the thin cotton of his cobalt-blue knit shirt, and she could feel the slightly springy texture of his chest hair beneath it. The faint smell of clean laundry underlaid by the aroma of a very masculine cologne filled her nostrils and trickled into her lungs.

"Listen, you oversized oaf." Libby made a determined effort to shut out her sense of smell, but that only made her more aware of the hard planes of his body where they pressed against her softer curves.

"It's no wonder you've never gotten a man to the point of asking you to marry him, if that's a sample of your conversation. Good Lord, woman, have you no concept of how to talk to a man? Try a little guile."

He tightened his grip and she felt her breasts crushed against his chest. The pressure sent a bubbling urgency ricocheting through her nervous system.

"I wouldn't demean your intelligence by using underhanded tactics." She tried to squirm away, but his arms held her tightly. His physical superiority roused no fear in her, merely excitement.

"Go ahead." He grinned at her, his white teeth gleaming in sharp relief against his deeply tanned skin. "Demean me a little."

Libby frowned repressively at him. As bullheaded as he was, she knew that if she didn't make the first move, he was perfectly capable of holding her this way indefinitely. And while he wasn't hurting her, the prolonged contact with his body was stoking her passion into a raging caldron of desire. A state that would quickly become apparent to him if she didn't escape soon.

She tilted her head back and glared up into his amused face. "Darlin' honeychile, big strong you wouldn't hurt li'l ole helpless me, would you?"

"Very good," he approved. "You're more adaptable than I thought."

"I have a strong sense of self-preservation!"

"And you deserve a reward."

"Reward? Do tell." She tilted her head back and looked at him. "You're going to cut out the Charles Atlas impersonations?"

"Better than that," he said a second before his head swooped downward, capturing her mouth.

Taken by surprise, her defenses were breached before she had an opportunity to rally them. His hard lips pressed and obeying the silent command she opened her mouth beneath his.

His large hand speared through her soft curls, holding her head immobile, and a shudder shook her frame as the velvety roughness of his tongue touched hers. Goose bumps erupted on her arms; warmth gathered in her loins, feeding her instinctive desire to respond to his caress.

Her hands slipped upward over his muscular shoulders to clasp his neck. The feel of his skin under her fingertips set up a gentle vibration throughout her body.

Mindlessly she pressed closer, feeling the hard outline of him burning into her soft thighs. The erotic sensation sent shock waves rippling through her, shattering her headlong response to him. He might have begun this kiss in a spirit of pure devilment, but it was obvious that he was no longer detached. Drawing on her deep sense of self-preservation, Libby jerked backward, taking him by surprise.

"Now what?" Joe sounded more amused than annoyed that she'd ended the embrace, which bolstered her feeling that she was doing the right thing.

"Forfeit over." She steadied her tremulous voice and went on. "I thought you were going to teach me how to bake a cake."

"There's all kinds of things I'd like to teach you." His seductive voice made her stomach curl in sensual excitement.

"I've got a library card. Be careful you aren't replaced by a cookbook," Libby said breathlessly.

"I'm much more versatile than a cookbook." His knowing smile promised untold delights, but to her relief he suddenly became very businesslike.

"Sit there." He pointed to the breakfast stool and she obediently climbed on it, laughing as he pulled a white chef's hat out of one of the sacks and put it on. It added at least six inches to his already tall body, making him appear enormous, especially when viewed against the backdrop of her small kitchen.

"Props," Libby chided as he wrapped a spotless white butcher's apron around his lean waist.

"Quiet, wench, genius requires concentration."

"But not modesty I take it." She began to enjoy herself. Somehow Joe, with his ridiculous hat, seemed perfectly at home in her kitchen.

"What kind of cake are we making?" she asked curiously.

"Frankfurter Kranz."

"Sounds like something you put mustard on."

"Philistine. But what can I expect from a woman who uses a box mix? This—" he lifted the lid from the cake carrier to reveal a large yellow tube cake "—is the base of the Frankfurter Kranz."

"You've already made it?"

"Yesterday. You have to let it set twenty-four hours before you can fill it. We'll make a second one tonight and you can try filling it yourself tomorrow."

"Thanks." Libby had no intention of fooling with a complicated filling. Any cake that wouldn't settle for a can of icing could go naked for all she cared.

"Now then—" he began to assemble his ingredients "—you set the oven to 325 degrees and coat this tube pan with butter, then flour it. You can do that, can't you?" He peered suspiciously at her.

"I'll give it my best shot." Her lips twitched at his engrossed expression. How could anyone take a cake so seriously, especially a grown man?

"I've got a mixer," she offered, as he began to smash the butter and sugar against the side of the bowl.

He didn't answer, merely looked down his nose at her and continued expending a great deal of unnecessary energy. Libby watched in fascination as the muscles in his right arm rippled with each beat. He was certainly more fun to watch than her mixer.

"What?" She blinked free of her daydreams to find Joe staring at her.

"I said," he repeated, "please pour out three-quarters of a cup of rum."

She picked up the dark bottle and whistled as she read the label. "This is pretty potent stuff. Three-quarters of a cup of this and you aren't going to be able to tell a box mix from your own."

"It's not for me." He frowned down into the mixture in the bowl and then gave it a few more whacks before pouring it into the pan she'd prepared. He dumped the mixing bowl in the sink and took a halfhearted swipe at the batter that had splashed on the counter. "It's for the cake we're going to fill. Open the oven door."

Libby pulled it open and watched him reverently slide the pan inside. He checked the dials while she poured the rum. Lowering her head until her eyes were level with the measuring cup, she squinted at the markings. A little too much.

She took a swallow, smiling as the dark, full flavor of the liquor hit the back of her throat. She looked again and frowned. She'd drank a bit too much. Carefully she tipped the bottle and added some more.

"What are you doing?" Joe demanded.

"Trying to get exactly three-quarters of a cup."

"You're going to get germs in my cake!"

"Nonsense." She took another tiny sip. "Nothing could live in all that alcohol."

"Give me that." He rescued the liquor, then pulled a wicked-looking knife with a blade of polished steel at least a foot long out of his sack. With a flick of his wrist he deftly sliced the cake crosswise into three equal layers.

Taking the rum, he sprinkled a quarter cup on each piece while she watched. Then he opened a container filled with a pale yellow mixture and began to spread it on the sections.

"What's that?" Libby stuck a finger in it and got her knuckles rapped with a wooden spoon for her troubles.

"The filling."

"It's good." She licked her finger. "What's in it?"

"Ten egg yolks, one pound unsalted butter, sugar, water and one-half cup of rum," he answered absently, carefully reassembling the layers.

"Good God, more rum! No wonder you turned your nose up at my poor mix. You like alcoholic cakes."

"I like distinction."

"At least my cakes can be served to the whole family. Yours are strictly for adults only."

"This cake isn't the only thing I do that's strictly for adults only." Joe gave her a slow grin, and her stomach twisted at the sensual promise in his voice.

"Let's concentrate on one thing at a time." She forced her mind back to the cake. If she wasn't careful he was going to realize how completely she was responding to him and her pride would never stand for that.

"Now for the topping." He began to press praline crumbs into the butter cream covering the sides and top of the cake.

"Pralines?" Libby snatched a morsel and popped it in her mouth, ignoring his indignant look. "There must be a million calories in that."

"You could do with a little more flesh," he grunted, ignoring her indignant gasp. "There." He stood back and studied his creation with pride.

Justifiable pride, she admitted. It looked like something out of an Austrian pastry shop.

"Perfect," he announced with no false modesty. "When you've cleaned up the kitchen we'll have a piece."

"When I've cleaned up the kitchen!" Libby gasped. "You're the one who made the mess." She looked around in dismay. Somehow in the course of his baking he'd managed to litter every available counter space with dirty dishes, dripping utensils and splashed cake batter.

"I am a chef." He drew himself up to his not inconsiderable height. "I don't do dishes."

"It's windows," she muttered nastily.

"I'll be in the living room going over some papers." Joe picked up the half-empty rum bottle and a glass. "Let me know when you're finished."

"Let you know . . . ?" Libby sputtered as the kitchen door swung shut behind him. He was serious. That wretched man actually expected her to clean up his mess. And he'd even taken the rum with him. A reluctant giggle escaped, to be followed by a rueful grin.

"I am a chef, indeed." When she got her hands on that contract, she most definitely intended to insert a clause stating he who messes up, cleans up. But for now, she admitted being beaten. If they had been at his place, she'd have simply walked out and left it, but that was hardly practical in her own home.

"Just you wait, Joe Landowski." She flipped on the hot water. "I'll get even with you for this."

5

LIBBY ROLLED OVER on the sofa, grabbed the ringing phone and muttered a drowsy hello into it.

"Libby?" Joe's crisp voice flooded her mind, shriveling the last remnants of sleep.

"Yes?" she answered around a yawn.

"You sound like you're asleep."

"Probably because I was."

"At three-thirty on a gorgeous Saturday afternoon?"

"I was correcting some math problems." She sat up, managing to knock over a stack of homework papers at the same time.

"That explains it," he commiserated. "Having to spend time on math would put anyone to sleep."

"Tell me, did you call simply to insult my profession or did you have an ulterior motive?" Her pleasure at hearing his voice was rapidly disintegrating under the impact of what his voice was saying.

"Yup. I have the revised contract."

"Six days. Not a bad turnaround."

"Even better was that they were six days without my father even once hinting at marriage," he said cheerfully.

"Same here. I had dinner at home last night and the subject of a husband never even came up. Although to be honest, it could have been because Mom was so taken with gambling that was all she could talk about."

"Gambling?" He laughed. "Let me guess. She discovered bingo?"

"Nothing so paltry. It seems that Dad finally gave in and took her to Atlantic City last weekend. And I have my suspicions as to why he suddenly went when he's refused to go for years," she added darkly. "At any rate, Mom won four thousand dollars in a slot machine."

Joe whistled in surprise. "Lucky."

"Yes, so now she sees herself as another Diamond Lil. I have the feeling that before Mom comes to her senses she's going to have blown the whole four thousand and a lot more besides. When I left she was indulging in the wholesale buying of lottery tickets."

"Maybe she'll get lucky again. Like the ad says, someone's going to win. It might as well be her."

"Someday I'll tell you the statistical probability of winning that thing."

"Don't bother." Joe chuckled. "I'm much happier in my ignorance. Anyway, since the contract came, I thought I'd call and see if you were free to go over it this evening."

Briefly Libby considered claiming a previous date just so he wouldn't think that no one wanted to go out with her, but common sense intruded. There was no reason for her to deny herself an evening in his company simply to give a false impression, when he wouldn't care anyway.

"Free as the proverbial bird," she said.

"Good." The satisfaction in his voice warmed her. "At the moment I'm working on a design problem with one of our new lines, but I'll have to quit shortly because I'm serving as lector at the five-thirty mass this evening. I'll pick you up at five and you can come to the services with me. Then, afterward, we'll have supper and we can work on the contract."

"Supper?" Libby asked cautiously, reluctant to get stuck with another mess in her kitchen.

"Mmm. There's a new restaurant that opened last week featuring Viennese cuisine. I wanted to try it out."

"Sounds good," she hastily agreed.

"Then I'll pick you up in an hour and a half?"

"Fine." She gently replaced the phone in the cradle and began absently to pick up her scattered papers while she considered what to wear. Joe hadn't said exactly what type of restaurant it was. It could be rigidly formal or it could be patterned after a Viennese tavern and consequently be very casual. If she overdressed, she might come across as too eager. No, better to err on the side of conservatism, she decided. She'd wear something appropriate for church.

She finished picking up the scattered math papers, dropped them on the coffee table and then wandered into the bathroom. A leisurely soak in a hot bath, she hoped, would put her in a relaxed frame of mind.

It didn't. Although the only reason Joe had invited her out was to negotiate the contract, her reasons for accepting were much more complex. She was strangely drawn to Joe Landowski, she admitted pensively as she finished drying her dripping body. She dropped the towel over the rack and frowned at the outfit she'd chosen.

Her eyes narrowed as she studied the classic Chanel lines of the sky-blue linen suit that she'd teamed with a chalk-white silk blouse with a soft tie. Myrna wouldn't have been caught dead wearing it, Libby acknowledged and then grimaced in disgust at the thought. What difference did it make what the gorgeous Myrna wore? She wasn't in competition with her. Nor did she want to be, she decided as she slipped on her lacy briefs.

"Not bad." Libby added the final touch of color to her soft lips. She might not be in Myrna's league, but she had something, she assured herself, moving into the living room to wait for Joe. She didn't have to wait long. At promptly five o'clock her doorbell rang and a sense of joyous anticipation filled her, the intensity of which vaguely appalled her. She had no business being this pleased to see him. After all, they were merely colleagues. And that only in the loosest sense. Think of him as a lawyer you're working with, she thought, giving herself some excellent advice.

A second assault on her doorbell ended her introspection and, hastily brushing back her curls, Libby hurried to open the door. She paused as she took in the exquisite tailoring of his three-piece gray suit and the somber magnificence of his navy silk tie.

"Hurry up," Joe ordered. "I'm double-parked and we haven't a minute to waste."

"Don't you ever say good evening? Or at least a simple 'hi there'?" She grabbed her purse as he rushed her out of the apartment.

"Why?" He punched the down button on the elevator.

"Observing the social amenities makes for a smoother-running world. Well, that's the theory anyway," she amended under his sardonic gaze.

Fortunately Joe's double-parking hadn't been discovered by a passing policeman and with a hasty, "Buckle up," he dumped her into the front seat.

Fifteen minutes later he maneuvered his silver Ferrari into a narrow space in the church's overflowing parking lot and hustled her out of the car.

"What's the hurry?" Libby demanded. "We've still got five minutes."

"I'm supposed to be in the vestry ten minutes before the mass starts. I told you I was reading."

"That's right." The recollection brought with it a slight sensation of dismay; he wasn't going to be sitting with her. Briskly she shook her head clear of the unwanted feeling and said, "You go in through the back of the church. It'll be quicker. I'll find myself a seat."

"Well . . ." He hesitated.

"Don't worry." Libby put the palm of her hand on the front of his suit jacket and gave him a gentle push. He didn't budge an inch.

"If you're sure . . ."

"Of course, I am. We career women are quite self-sufficient." She was unable to resist the gibe.

"Maddening, too," he muttered, hurrying toward the rear entrance.

Leave it to him to get in the last word. She sighed in resignation and entered the church, blinking to accustom her eyes to the dim lighting. After she dipped her fingers in the holy water and crossed herself, she looked around for an empty seat. There was one to the right of the center aisle and she quickly slipped into it.

Almost on cue, the organ swelled in a joyous litany of praise, and Libby relaxed as a feeling of peace stole over her. The congregation rose as one when the procession started down the center aisle. She watched as Joe followed the two priests to the alter and then went to stand at the lectern. He seemed different somehow. As the priest began the opening prayer, she surreptitiously studied Joe. All signs of the laughing, teasing man she'd come to know over the past week had disappeared. The fanciful thought occurred to her that this Joe was more like one of the Old Testament prophets. She sank back against the hard wooden pew.

The fact that he was taking an active role in the service didn't really surprise her. Judging from what she'd already learned about him, he was a man who would support what he believed in with his time as well as his money. He had a solid inner core. He could be counted on to stand by any commitments he made. Not that she was looking for a commitment from him, Libby hastily assured herself. All she wanted from Joe was some help in diverting her father. That and dinner. She tuned out the meandering sermon the priest had embarked upon and tried to decide what she'd order. She was starved.

She still hadn't decided by the time they arrived at the restaurant. Curiously, she glanced around as they waited by an ornate sign that informed them a hostess was on duty. The restaurant was naturally dark, having few windows, and the situation was not improved by the walnut paneling that covered the lower two-thirds of the walls. Above the wood, the cream plaster walls were studded with a variety of mounted horns.

"What do you think?" Joe noticed her interest in the decorating.

"At least they didn't stuff the heads, too," she offered.

"The effect's very Austrian, though. The whole decor reminds me of Figlmuller's in Vienna. Even to the highly polished wooden tables."

"And the lack of a hostess?" She glanced around the crowded room.

"I think that's her." He nodded toward a harried-looking young woman in a Tyrolean peasant costume who was rushing toward them.

"Sorry to keep you waiting." The woman apologized, her gaze lingering on Joe's chiseled features as she smoothed the full green skirt down over her shapely hips. "The salad girl called in sick at the last minute and I'm trying to lend a hand in between customers."

"That's all right," Libby said, tired of being ignored. She wasn't used to hostesses eyeing her escorts as if they were the blue plate special. . . . But then she'd never had an escort that looked quite like Joe.

"If you'll just follow me." The woman tore her gaze away from Joe and began to thread a path through the crowded room. She paused beside a table for two set under a large gilt mirror and handed them two mimeographed sheets. "The menus haven't come from the printer yet," she apologized. "Your waitress will be along shortly."

"Thank you." Joe smiled at her, and with a last regretful look at him, she left.

Libby studied the sheet.

"What would you like?" he asked.

"Why?" she asked suspiciously.

"Because I want to order something different. That way we can sample two dishes."

"I think I'll have the broiled lamb in marjoram sauce."

"Then I'll try the Backhendl. Fried chicken," he elaborated at her puzzled look. "It's the Austrian culinary symbol of upper-class prosperity."

"Fried chicken?" She giggled. "The colonel would be honored."

"It's not just any fried chicken," he said in all seriousness. "It's seasoned, coated three times and fried for fifteen minutes in hot lard, then served with a wedge of lemon. Or, sometimes, fried parsley. But this isn't the traditional atmosphere." He glanced around the crowded, noisy room. "Backhendl should be served in a garden on a warm summer's night with a chilled white wine. Like Gumpoldskirchner."

"Drink New York State wine. We have some of the best in the world. Not only that, but you can pronounce the names."

"Yes, but—"

"But nothing. We should support our own industries."

"Isolationist," he muttered, turning to the distracted-looking waitress, who was wearing an elaborate costume similar to that of the hostess except hers had a headdress that was obviously bothering her.

The young woman tossed her head to shake dangling beads out of her line of vision and scribbled their order. Then with a distracted look over her shoulder, she scurried away.

"Understaffed." Libby stated the obvious.

"Mmm." Joe seemed unconcerned. "All new restaurants have teething problems. The crucial factor will be whether the cook is equal to the occasion."

When the waitress placed her dinner in front of her, Libby admitted that whoever was in the kitchen was probably a genius. Thick slices of lamb, smothered with a light gravy, were topped with julienne strips of parsnips, carrots and celery, while sliced potatoes surrounded the dish.

"It looks delicious and smells even better," Libby told the waitress who was gently placing a plate of golden fried chicken down in front of Joe.

"Yes, our cook—" The woman turned toward Libby. Unfortunately the action shook loose one of the strands on her headdress, flinging it into the middle of Joe's dish of vegetables.

"Oh dear!" the woman gasped. "I'm so sorry."

"Don't be." Joe gave her a slow smile as he picked it out. "It'll make a delightful souvenir of the occasion. I doubt you're going to need it much longer. Those headdresses are bound to go."

"I sure hope so." The woman sighed. "I'm tired of being whacked in the face every time I turn around. I'll have some more veggies for you in a second." She picked up his dish and hurried away, returning a few seconds later with a fresh one.

"This really is delicious." Libby munched on the succulent meat. "How's yours?"

"Excellent." Joe cut off a piece of chicken and placed it on her plate. "Try for yourself."

Obediently she tried it. "Very good," she pronounced, glancing up to see him staring at her lamb.

"Was that a gentle hint for a taste of mine?" She laughed. "If you don't mind."

"Of course not." She stabbed a slice of lamb and dropped it on his plate. "The servings are quite large and I want to save room to sample dessert."

"Most definitely," he agreed seriously. "Austrian pastries are some of the best in the world."

As well as some of the most caloric, Libby thought ruefully as she savored the last crumb of her Sacher torte. She placed her fork on her empty plate and began to sip her coffee, which had a huge glob of whipped cream floating in it.

"That was delicious. Thank you for bringing me."

"My pleasure." Joe speared the last cognac-soaked strawberry from his Spanische Windtorte and ate it. "New restaurants don't always make it, but I think this one is destined to be a success once they work out a few minor problems." He touched the string of beads lying beside his coffee cup with a large forefinger.

"Shall we go back to my place?" she asked.

"No, I left the contract at my apartment and I also set the timer on the coffee maker before I left, so we'll have fresh coffee when we get there."

"You're going to make some girl a marvelous househusband." She grinned, ignoring his grimace.

"Come on—" He picked up the check. "I want to leave plenty of time for negotiations. Several clauses need extensive revisions."

"You can say that again," she muttered as she allowed him to shepherd her out of the restaurant.

Libby breathed a sigh of pleasure as she sank down into the welcoming depths of Joe's oversize down-filled sofa. She studied his huge living room with interest. It was every bit as luxurious as she remembered. Now that she wasn't consumed with anger, details that she'd missed the first time she'd been here became apparent. Her attention was caught by what appeared to be a collection of Meissen china in an antique cherry cabinet. Her approving gaze lit on the muted red tones of the Kasim prayer rug hanging on the wall beside it. Somehow it complemented the modernistic painting behind the sofa.

"Here you are." Joe handed her a mug of steaming coffee and then slipped off his suit jacket, vest and tie and carelessly dropped them on the brown Eames lounger.

"Thanks." Libby took a sip of the scalding brew before setting it on the lamp table to cool.

"How did your design problem go?" she asked idly as she watched him rifle through the mounds of paper littering the coffee table.

"It didn't," he responded absently, ignoring a huge stack of computer printout that toppled off to spill across the dense amber pile of the carpet.

"Ha, it's nice to know that you're lacking at least one of the housewifely virtues." She sank down on the carpet and began to pick the printout up.

"What's that?" he murmured, still making a mess of the papers.

"Neatness."

"I create," he announced loftily. "Wives . . ." He paused as if reconsidering what he'd been about to say.

"Very wise." She set the printout back on the table. "A crack like that could get you picketed."

"Don't mention pickets." He shuddered. "It's too reminiscent of labor problems."

"Do you have many?"

"No." He sifted through another stack. "Most garment workers are fully cognizant of the problems represented by the flood of cheap clothing imports pouring into this country. Clothing that's cheap because for the most part it's made in sweatshop conditions." His voice deepened with the strength of his feelings.

"Down, boy," Libby soothed. "I promise I'll check for a union label before I ever buy another thing."

"You should," he said seriously. "Cheap imports because of subsistence wages are a big problem in many areas. Not just clothing." He dropped the last stack of papers on the coffee table and glanced around distractedly. "What did I do with that thing?"

Libby, correctly assuming that the question was not aimed at her, stuck to the original subject.

"What exactly do you manufacture? I vaguely remember you saying something about your father being a garment maker."

"Uh-huh. He was a tailor in Poland. And when he emigrated he began to manufacture a line of high-quality ladies' lingerie."

"Underwear!" She laughed uproariously, for some reason finding the thought of Joe surrounded by silk and satin undergarments very funny. He was such a thoroughly masculine specimen that the contrast was ludicrous.

"Originally," he said stiffly, "but over the years we've branched out into other fields. We have a very successful line of women's sportswear, a line of women's natural fiber coats, a line aimed at the active sportsperson, and we're in the process of developing a line of children's wear."

"Underwear!" She chortled, totally ignoring the rest.

"There's nothing funny about making ladies' wear," he said tightly.

"If you say so." She continued to giggle, a fact that he definitely did not find amusing.

"Liberty Joy Michalowski!" His large hands grasped the slight bones of her shoulders and he gave her a gentle shake.

"Sorry." She pressed her lips together to control her laughter. "But you were pretty free with the cracks about my profession and everyone in it. What's the matter? Can't you take what you dish out?"

"Oh, I can take it." A gleam of some emotion flared deep within his azure eyes. "The question, my irreverent friend, is can you?" He pushed and Libby suddenly found herself lying on her back on the dense carpeting with his large body looming above her.

Her tongue darted out to lick her dry lips. "Why do I have the feeling that I missed something?" she whispered.

"Rest assured, Libby, you aren't going to miss a thing." His face came closer and she tried to concentrate on the fine lines radiating from his eyes in an attempt to block out the insidious pull he was exerting on her senses. Laugh lines, her mind labeled them. But this was no laughing matter, she realized in dismay. Her body was awakening to tingling life where his heavy frame touched hers, and a burgeoning warmth was blossoming in her abdomen. Her sensitivity to his touch was growing with each additonal exposure, not abating as she'd hoped.

"I don't think—"

"I've noticed that," he interrupted. "You remind me of one of my foremen who described his son as 'book-learning smart and living stupid.'"

She opened her mouth to defend herself at the instant his hard lips captured hers. His warm breath invaded her mouth, sending tiny sparks of desire shooting down to her lungs where they seemed to coalesce into one giant ball of heated desire.

His fingers began to trace insubstantial patterns over the soft skin of her cheek. She moaned against his mouth as he continued his tactile stimulation, moving up her jawline and dipping into the curve of her ear.

Libby's hands clasped his broad shoulders and she dug her heels into the soft carpeting, arching her body into his. The knot of desire in her loins tightened as she felt the pressure of his hard muscles. She reacted mindlessly when his tongue plunged into her mouth in a burst of masculine domination, his caress sending shivers coursing over her skin. Her hands convulsively clutched his muscular neck.

Suddenly his large hands engulfed her smaller ones and brought them to her sides. "The bedroom," he announced triumphantly.

"No," she gasped, instinctively knowing that going to bed with him would create more problems than it would solve. Her body might crave closer contact with his with a fervor that ignored reason and common sense, but her mind knew it was a bad idea.

"I'm sure that's where I left it." Joe levered himself upward with a lithe grace.

"Left it?" she repeated in confusion.

"The contract. The one I was looking for. I just remembered that I left it in my bedroom. Wait here. I'll be back in a second."

"Sure." Her pride cut through the confused mass of unresolved yearnings churning through her body. He seemed to have emerged from their brief embrace with no aftereffects, while she . . . Libby glanced down at her hand, grimacing at the fine tremors shaking it. She was finding it difficult even now to free herself of the effects.

She got up, straightened her skirt and reached for her coffee. It was imperative that Joe not realize how much his casual kisses had upset her equilibrium. Especially since the effect was not reciprocal.

6

"I WAS RIGHT." Joe was back in two minutes, looking very pleased with himself. "That was where I left it."

He sat down on the floor beside the coffee table, stretched out his long legs and leaned back against the sofa, where Libby was now sitting.

Surreptitiously she moved away from his back, which was almost touching her legs. She didn't want any more physical contact with him. At least not until she'd recovered from their last encounter, she thought ruefully. He picked up his cup of coffee and began to sip idly as he read the neatly typed document.

"How did it arrive?" she asked curiously. "By special messenger again?"

"I'm not sure." He turned the page. "I found it under the door when I got home from work last night."

And he'd waited until today to call her, Libby thought, wondering where he'd been last night. Had he made up with the luscious Myrna despite what he'd said earlier? A quiver of dismay took her by surprise.

"I almost missed it. It was after eleven before we finally gave up on the design problem and I was so tired, I didn't even see the contract until I tripped over it."

"Oh?" Libby was disheartened by the intensity of the feeling of relief that filled her.

"Let me see." He tapped the stubby eraser against his strong, white teeth as he studied the first paragraph. "I think I'm missing something here."

"You're missing a lot of things if we're talking about you ideas on women and marriage!"

"Didn't those brides used to bring hope chests full of stuf to the marriage?"

"As long as it's not cows," she said sourly, rememberin Dave Talbot's unfortunate analogy.

"Bed linens and real embroidered tablecloths." He scrib bled in the margin.

"Do you have any idea of the amount of work involved i embroidering one of those things?"

"What better way to keep a girl busy?"

"How about making voodoo dolls of male chauvinists? Libby said darkly.

He ignored her. "My grandmother had a picnic cloth al most covered with red embroidery. I think that's what want." He made another notation on the side.

"Then want will be your master!"

"You'll get your chance at the contract." He repeated he earlier words smugly. "Now then, how many sets of bed line should I ask for?"

"Three."

"Only three?"

"Sure. One for the bed, one for the wash and one for th closet."

"No." He shook his head. "You're supposed to have a whol chest full. Enough to last a long time. Say an even dozen." H added it to the contract.

"Twelve!" she gasped. "Your sheet supply will last longe than most marriages."

"Not mine." His relaxed features unexpectedly took on serious cast. "I don't believe in divorce. The trouble with to many marriages today is that at the first sign of trouble, th couple throw in the towel and look for a new partner. My wif isn't going to be given that option."

"To heck with the towel. She'll probably throw you in!"

"Nonsense. I plan on being the perfect husband."

She choked on her coffee. "You couldn't be a perfect husband if you were comatose!"

"I should think not." He gave her a wolfish grin. "One of my best roles is that of lover."

"I wouldn't know about that," Libby remarked, wisely retreating.

"Of course you wouldn't. I'm not courting you. What about a feather mattress?"

"What about it?" she asked in confusion.

"I want my bride to bring a feather mattress to the marriage."

"Do they even make such things anymore?"

"My great-grandmother plucked the geese to make her own."

"I see. Insanity runs in the family, does it?"

"There's no reason to be envious of my great-grandmother. I'm sure you'll think of something."

"Oh, I've thought of lots of things where you're concerned. It's just that they're all either illegal or immoral."

"Immoral?" Joe looked up with interest. "Tell me about them."

"Well, murder and mayhem top the list," she said dryly.

"I have much more interesting ideas when it comes to immorality."

"I don't doubt it. I did see the luscious Myrna."

"She was, wasn't she?" he said reflectively. "But she wasn't very bright. You couldn't talk to her."

"I'm surprised you tried. I thought your complaint about me was that I was smart."

"Too smart," he corrected her. "There's a lot of ground between your intelligence and Myrna's lack of it. But that's beside the point. I want a feather mattress and twelve sets of sheets."

"And a partridge in a pear tree."

"Now then—" he thoughtfully chewed the eraser "—about your job. Or, more specifically, your ridiculous insistence on keeping it."

"It is not ridiculous!"

"I can support you in a style that the vast majority of women would love to become accustomed to."

"Tell me—" Libby frowned at him "—if you liquidated your assets, what would you realize?"

Joe looked thoughtful. "Quite a lot. I own all the property our plants sit on, including the office building in Manhattan that houses our showrooms."

"Just give me a round figure."

"About eight to ten million, depending on the state of the real estate market at the time of the sale. Why?"

"Because that leads to a very logical question. Why don't you liquidate your assets, invest the proceeds and live off the income?"

"That's ridiculous."

"No, it isn't. You'd have more money to spend than you do now."

"But what would I do all day?"

"What do you want me to do all day?" she countered.

"That's different," he insisted. "You'd be responsible for running the house and overseeing the kids. That should provide enough scope for anyone."

"Why don't you put your money where your mouth is?" Libby eyed him narrowly as an idea began to form in the back of her mind."

"Exactly what does that mean?"

"It means that you shouldn't give out advice until you've tried it."

"What do you expect me to do? Dissolve a thriving business and put a lot of people out of work simply to prove a point?"

"No, I'm not unreasonable."

"You could have fooled me," he said under his breath.

"What I had in mind was for you to give the exalted role of motherhood a trial run, so to speak. You feel that being a housewife and mother is adequate stimulation. Then you try it. A week from Tuesday our parish school is going to do an inventory and my cousin Elizabeth said she'd help if she could find a baby-sitter. Why don't you take the day off work and look after her four boys? I could bring them by before I go to work in the morning and you can be the one in charge of the house, the boys, the meals, the whole lot. Give your housekeeper the day off. I'll come back here after my last class, and then we can take the boys home."

"Sounds like a snap."

What would snap would be his patience and possibly his sanity, she thought gleefully, not feeling the least bit of remorse for what she was letting him in for. He thought being a wife and mother was a sinecure; let him try it.

"But I can only do it if I manage to get my design problem solved," he warned.

"You were the one who said that we were supposed to negotiate as if this were for real! Now what's more important, some design or your future wife?"

"Well . . ."

"Small wonder no woman's been willing to take you on. Besides, if you still haven't solved your problem by then, a break would probably help."

"Perhaps," he said cautiously. "I have been working rather hard lately. A nice relaxing day at home would be nice."

Libby took a sip of her coffee, hiding the grin that split her face. A nice relaxing day indeed! Just wait until he made the acquaintance of her four young cousins. A gleeful sense of anticipation filled her.

"But I want something in return," he said. "Once I prove how rewarding housekeeping is, you have to agree to stay home. That's only fair."

"Fair?" She choked. "You want to trade one day for my entire future!"

"Then what's the point of my doing it?" he demanded.

"I want you to get an appreciation of what a wife and mother actually goes through. Then, maybe, you won't be so intractable about having a stay-at-home wife."

"Maybe," he said doubtfully, "but it seems to me that your experiment is more likely to simply reinforce what I've been trying to tell you."

"We'll see."

"Well, while we're seeing, I'm putting in a demand for a nonworking wife." He slashed out her counterproposal from last Saturday.

"Now then, about where we'll live . . ."

"Long Island is out," she insisted.

"How about Connecticut?"

"New York City. No commute!"

"But I keep telling you that children need room to play in order to develop normally."

"Are you trying to tell me that every single kid who's growing up in the city is abnormal?" she asked incredulously. "Come to think of it, where did you live when you were a kid?"

"East Sixty-fifth Street."

"Ha! Maybe I was too hasty. Maybe you're right."

"Very funny." Joe dismissed her humor. "But I will admit that you have a point."

"And I'll admit that you also have one," she responded seriously. "Of course there's a great deal of validity in what you're saying. A big grassy yard would be nice for the kids. But when the price for it is two hours less time a day with their parents, it's simply too dearly bought."

"But if you didn't work—"

"You have a one-track mind!" she interrupted him. "Let's leave my career out of it for a minute and just consider you. What time do you normally start work?"

"I like to go over the day's schedule before everyone else gets in. Usually about eight-thirty. Why?"

"Think a minute. To get to the city from Long Island by eight-thirty, it'll take a car trip to the train station, say fifteen minutes. An hour on the commuter train, plus at least another twenty minutes to get from Grand Central Station to your office. That's an hour and thirty-five minutes one way. To get to your office by eight-thirty, you'll have to leave the house by six fifty-five at the latest. Probably long before the children are awake. What time do you leave now?"

"About eight-ten."

"Hmm." She nodded. "That would give you time to have breakfast with that flock of kids you're so keen on. Now let's look at the other end. What time do you leave work?"

"Around five-thirty."

"So if you lived on the island, then you'd arrive back home after seven when small children are ready for bed. Good Lord, Joe, you're never going to see these kids. They're going to grow up thinking that you're a weekend visitor. Is that what you want?"

"No." He gave her a curiously penetrating stare. "You're right. I never considered it from that angle before."

"Well, do it now because I guarantee you that when your children look back on their childhood they aren't going to remember the grass. What they'll remember is their absentee father."

"What you're saying makes a lot of sense." He squinted thoughtfully as he considered her words. "Living in the city is probably the best choice, given the alternatives."

"You think so?" Libby blinked uncertainly. Somehow she'd never expected him to give an inch.

"Certainly. Despite my lack of formal education, I do have my share of common sense. I'll agree that we should live in the city." He made a notation on the contract. "However, since we now will have so much more time on our hands, there shouldn't be any problem with our having six kids."

"No problem!" she snorted, "I'm thirty years old. Even if I agreed to have six kids and we started immediately, I'd practically have to have them every year."

"Really, Libby," Joe scoffed, "for a mathematician, you certainly aren't very accurate. We could certainly wait eighteen months between children."

"Oh, big deal!" she sputtered. "You honestly expect any woman to have six kids eighteen months apart? And at my age?"

"Well, you're not getting any younger."

"No, but I'm going to get very old, very fast if you have your way."

"I'd love to have my way with you." His twinkling eyes focused on her lips with an almost tangible force.

"Don't play word games with me!" Libby snapped, unnerved by his teasing suggestion. Logic might tell her that he didn't mean it, but her imagination was busily painting images across her emotions. Images of his heavy body pressed against hers. Images of his hair-roughened legs between hers. Images of . . . She forced herself to black out the disturbing thoughts.

"All right, maybe you are too old for six," he grudgingly agreed. "I'll lower my expectations to five."

"Try sinking them to two!"

"Five and not a kid less."

"Two and, besides, what happens if I don't conceive that easily?"

"Persistence pays off in these kinds of things." He grinned at her.

"I'll bet." She wisely dropped the subject.

"It's settled then. Five kids." He scribbled on the contract.

"The only thing that's settled is that you're being entirely unrealistic," she said tartly. "I certainly haven't agreed to anything."

"You'll get your turn when the contract comes back to you." He noticed her empty cup. "Want another cup of coffee?"

"No, thanks." Libby shook her head. "Let's finish up. I'm a little tired."

"Beginning to feel your advanced age?" he teased.

"It's been a bad week." She ignored the crack. "My graduate assistant has the flu, and I've been trying to correct all the homework myself."

"Your students having troubles?"

"I can't understand their work enough to tell." She sighed. "It's like trying to read hieroglyphics. On top of that my doctoral student thinks that simply because I'm a woman, he should be able to tell me what to do. The pompous jackass," she grumbled. "I finally told him to either do it my way or find himself another advisor."

"Did that put the fear of God into him?"

"Who knows." She shrugged. "He stormed out of my office threatening dire consequences and I haven't seen him since."

"Consequences?" Joe's face tautened. "Like what?"

"If I understand correctly, his daddy is going to complain to the president of the university. Or was it his mother?" Libby frowned.

"His daddy!"

"Hmm." She nodded. "His daddy's a hot-shot congressman from somewhere out west. Apparently sonny hasn't as yet adjusted to the fact that he's outside daddy's bailiwick."

"You had me worried there for a minute."

"Don't be. Academia has its share of back stabbers, but they're strictly metaphorical."

"I still don't like it."

"It's a fact of life. Despite what most people think, universities are just as prone to politics as offices."

"No, I mean your graduate student."

"I don't, either. But I can get rid of him, and if he doesn't shape up, I will."

"You surprise me. I wouldn't have thought that you had a ruthless bone in your body."

"When have you ever really seen me? You've simply imposed your rather distorted image of femininity on me."

"Oh, I've seen you. And everything I've seen tells me that you are basically a kind, reasonable person. Even as angry as you were last Friday when you practically forced your way in here, you were willing to listen to my explanation. And even though your father's actions had made you the butt of your colleagues' jokes, you could still see his side."

"That's different. My personal life is one thing. My professional life is another thing entirely. In personal relationships one has to compromise, but one never compromises one's professional integrity."

"Maybe in a man . . ." he began, only to pause under the force of Libby's glare.

"Quit while you're ahead," she warned "or I'm liable to give you a demonstration of ruthlessness that'll destroy your perception of me forever."

"Impossible," Joe announced with a slight smile, "but you're right about one thing. It's too late to get into a fight. We'll wait till another time."

"Wonderful, something to look forward to." She stood up, stretched and yawned, missing the way his eyes gleamed as her silk blouse stretched over her small breasts. "Have you put your last unreasonable piece of dogma into that thing?"

"Almost." He frowned. "I have one more thing to add about kids."

"As long as it's not another one." She sat on the arm of the sofa.

"No." He scribbled away in the margin. "I want the children baptized and raised in the Catholic faith."

"For once we're in agreement." She gave him a look of mock astonishment. "But since I'm Catholic, too, I fail to see why it's even necessary to mention it."

"I wouldn't have thought it necessary to mention that I wanted a stay-at-home wife and mother," he retorted. "After all, with your background, it should have been a foregone conclusion."

"Have you ever considered importing a bride? If you really worked at it, you might be able to find a village somewhere in rural Poland where they still abide by the old ways."

"The last thing is about education." Joe went on, ignoring her remark. "The kids are to go to a Catholic school."

"Why?"

"I did."

"That's not much of a recommendation. Although I suppose it's unfair of me to blame a whole church for the way you turned out."

"That's 'give credit' for the way I turned out," he corrected as he continued writing. "I happen to feel that it's very important for the schools to reinforce the values being taught at home. Especially in this day and age."

"You don't need the reinforcement if you're doing it right, and, conversely, if you're doing a bad job the school can't inculcate values for you."

"No, but it can't hurt. Did you read the latest report on the state of education in the U.S.?"

"Of course I read it. I'm an educator and to some extent I agreed with it. But when all's said and done, the schools are merely reflecting what society wants. We've put a whole lot more on the schools than merely teaching the basics."

"I'm not interested in placing blame; I'm merely interested in avoiding the results."

"That's ridiculous! New York City has some fine public schools."

"It also has some very bad ones and I'm not willing to take the risk with my kids." He tossed the revised manuscript on the coffee table and stood up. "Come on. I'll run you home."

"Okay," Libby agreed, rather disappointed at his summary ending of the evening even though she had to admit it was her own fault. She had been the one to bring up going home first.

"LIBBY, I NEED YOU to do me a favor tonight. It's Wednesday." Jessie closed Libby's front door behind her.

"I don't know how those two things are related, but you can tell me in the kitchen. I'm icing a cake."

"Sure." Jessie trailed along behind her, climbing up onto a breakfast stool. She glanced at the chocolate cake Libby was spreading apricot preserves on. "What's that?"

"A Sacher torte." Libby put the two layers together and, picking up the pan simmering over hot water on the stove, began to pour the chocolate mixture over the cake. Instead of coating it the way it was supposed to, most of the icing ran off the sides to form puddles on the counter.

"Not enough powdered sugar?" Jessie hazarded a guess.

"Not enough something." Libby began to scoop it up and dump it back on top and it promptly slid off again. "Damn! It's not supposed to do that."

"I've got a can of icing you can have," Jessie offered.

"It's the principle of the thing." Libby determinedly scraped the icing off the counter and slapped it back on the cake.

"What principle?"

"That that man can do it and I can't. Do you know—" Libby licked the glaze off her sticky fingers "—he made the most incredible rum cake last week. I took part of it to my mother and she didn't stop raving all afternoon. And she didn't even know it had been made by some guy I'm supposed to be dating."

"Ah, the other half of the contract cooks," Jessie guessed.

"Like a professional," Libby admitted. "And if some man can cook like that, I don't see why I can't."

"Liberty Joy Michalowski!" Jessie hooted. "Of all the sexist remarks!"

"What?" Libby looked up, a confused expression on her face.

"Your crack that simply because you're a woman you should be a better cook."

"But he gloats," Libby stated obscurely.

"Try the refrigerator."

"He wouldn't fit. Besides, how's that going to cure gloating?"

"No, for that stuff you call icing."

"Think it'll work?"

"It works on fudge that won't set, and it certainly can't be any worse than it already is."

"True," Libby conceded. She finished scraping the icing, put the pan in the refrigerator and wiped her sticky countertop.

"Speaking of Joseph Landowski, how are the negotiations going?"

"Hard to tell," Libby admitted. "We worked on the contract last Saturday over at his place, but I haven't heard from him since."

"It's been four days. Why don't you call him up and ask about it?"

"Because it comes here next."

"So, call him anyway. It's permissible."

"You may know that and I may know that, but does Joe?" Libby rinsed out her dishcloth and began to scrub the dirty pots.

"What do you mean?" Jessie asked.

"I'm not sure." Libby looked pensive. "Joe Landowski is a very unusual mixture."

"I'll say." Jessie chortled. "I've never seen a man as gorgeous as he is even in the movies. The good fairies must have been having a convention when he was baptized."

"He's not that spectacular."

"You need glasses."

"No, I need earplugs."

"What?"

"It isn't how he looks, it's what he says," Libby clarified.

"Don't tell me. That gorgeous hunk is a male chauvinist? I knew he looked to good to be true."

"Not exactly." Libby rinsed a pot as she tried to find the right words to explain. "He's not precisely a chauvinist."

"Then what is he?"

"Maybe a traditionalist." Libby frowned. "As near as I can tell he's not against women working. He's only against his own wife working."

"Ahh." Jessie nodded sagely. "I've run across those before."

"I haven't. It's rather disconcerting to find a man with two sets of standards for something besides sex. Especially when I'm not sure where I stand with him."

"I know where I'd like to stand with him." Jessie giggled. "Or better yet, where I'd like to lay with him. I'll bet he'd be dynamite to kiss. All those lovely muscles." She sighed rapturously.

"Umm." Libby turned back to the sink, unwilling to discuss the subject. Those kisses she'd exchanged with Joe were private and not to be shared with even a good friend like Jessie.

"How does he treat you?" Jessie's curiosity was obviously aroused.

"Like a friend of the family."

"That doesn't sound like much fun."

"It has it's moments," Libby allowed, and then hurried on. "In the beginning he was emphatic about the importance of pretending the negotiations were real, but even so, sometimes I get the distinct impression that he's forgotten it's not a real contract."

"Role emersion," Jessie pointed out sagely.

"And I forget, too," Libby admitted. "Every time he starts yelling about my quitting work and staying home to raise his kids, I see red."

Libby let the water out of the sink, then added thoughtfully, "Actually, though, it hasn't all been in vain. Do you know that I spent all Sunday afternoon with my mother and not once did she grill me on whom I was seeing. Not only that, but she was actually knitting a sweater for my Uncle Pawel."

"So?" Jessie looked confused.

"My mother has this half-finished baby sweater she usually knits when I'm around. It's her subtle way of reminding me that she still doesn't have any grandchildren.... And stop laughing. It's not funny." Libby glared at the chuckling Jessie.

"I can't help it; it's priceless."

"No, it's maddening," Libby corrected. "But, at any rate, this contract has given me the first peace I've had since I graduated from college."

"Then it's worth it."

"Yes," Libby agreed, wondering if it was. Maybe she was simply exchanging one set of problems for another. Deep in her heart she wondered if Joe didn't represent a greater threat to her peace of mind than her parents' nagging ever had. But she brushed the idea aside, telling herself that he simply disturbed her because his ideas were so annoying.

"Actually, Libby, what I came over for was to see if you could sit in my apartment from seven till about seven-thirty."

"Sure." Libby glanced at the clock on the wall. "What do you want done?"

"Just be there. Someone from the law firm called. They've managed to get a hold of a deposition that I really need, and one of the law clerks is going to drop it off on his way home. But tonight's my regular night to man the phone at the crisis center, and I hate to disappoint them at the last minute."

"No problem. I can correct papers at your place as well as I can here."

"Thanks, Libby, I really appreciate it."

"YOU'RE LATE." Sigismund looked reprovingly at Frederic as he sank down into the empty chair and heaved a sigh.

"The copier at the library was broken and I had the devil of a time finding another place to Xerox the contract. Is this mine?" He looked hopefully at the drink in front of him.

Casimir nodded. "We went ahead and ordered for you."

"So?" Sigismund demanded once Frederic had taken a deep sip of the reviving whisky. "Why did it take them so long to negotiate the latest version? This is Thursday and we returned it to them last Friday."

"Patience, Sigismund, patience. That's not even a whole week." Frederic handed copies of the contract to the two waiting men.

Casimir squinted at him and fumbled in his jacket pocket for his bifocals.

"Mmm." Sigismund quickly glanced over it.

"Discouraging, isn't it?" Frederic sighed. "Can you imagine them wasting time discussing linen?"

"An embroidered picnic tablecloth." Casimir smiled as he reminisced. "My grandmother had one."

"Unfortunately, so did Joe's!" Frederic snapped. "Which is undoubtedly where the idea came from."

"A feather mattress!" Sigismund read incredulously.

Casimir looked at him over the top of his glasses. "At least they're talking."

"True," Frederic agreed. "But I can't help but wonder why they're going along with the negotiations. Do you suppose it's possible that they really are willing to be guided by older and wiser heads . . . ? Well, it was just a thought," he added defensively at the other two's stares.

"I'm not positive," Sigismund said thoughtfully, "but I think this comes under the heading of busywork."

"What's that?" Frederic asked.

"Meaningless work given to keep someone occupied and out of mischief. I used to give it to my classes occasionally."

"Occupied!" Frederic was outraged.

"You must admit it was effective." Casimir chuckled. "You were even late to lunch because you couldn't find a place to get it copied."

"Ha!" Frederic took a healthy gulp of his whisky. "It would have served them right if I'd had it done at a place where anyone could read it."

"Don't get discouraged," Casimir said. "I have the strong feeling that they may find themselves caught in their own brilliant plan."

"I think you may be right." Sigismund nodded reflectively. "Take a look at that first paragraph. They've managed to agree to live in New York City."

"That's the only thing they've agreed on," Frederic said.

"In it's entirety, yes," Casimir agreed. "But notice how they both seem to be giving a little in the other areas. Joe's agreed to pay a housekeeper for cleaning, and Libby's raised the ante from one to two kids."

"Yes, and take a look at that paragraph." Sigismund tapped it with a thin forefinger. "We didn't have anything in the original about education. That was their own idea. It's an encouraging sign that they're expanding the contract into other areas."

"True. I told you it was working." Frederic beamed.

"At the moment," Casimir concurred. "But our hold on them is tenuous to say the least, so don't try anything else."

"Anything else?" Sigismund blinked.

"Any other matchmaking. Of any sort," Casimir added emphatically, seeing the look on Frederic's face. "If we're right, our only hold is that while we're negotiating the contract they're getting a respite from you two and your matchmaking. So to try matchmaking would convince them there's no point in continuing."

"You could be right," Sigismund mused.

"But what about the bed linen?"

"To hell with the linen, what about the bed?"

"It would serve them right if we really gave them a feather mattress," Casimir asserted.

"Yes, it would." Frederic's faded blue eyes took on a wicked glint. "They might be a little more careful in the future."

"You have an idea?" Sigismund asked.

"Hmm." Frederic nodded. "I have a contact in the industry who supplies chicken feathers for pillows. I'm sure he'd give me enough to fill a mattress ticking." He looked questioningly at the other two. "Should we?"

"Definitely," they chorused.

"After all—" Sigismund managed to look angelic "—we're only giving them what they said they wanted."

"True." The other two nodded self-righteously.

7

By Friday it was obvious to Libby that there would be no surprise visit from Joe that week. Nor had he phoned, which left her with no choice but to wait until the contract had been delivered before contacting him herself. Or until Monday when she could call, using the excuse that she was checking to see if he was still willing to take her young cousins for the day.

"Here, let me." Jessie sprinted down the hallway and grabbed the sack of groceries Libby was attempting to wedge between her thigh and the wall while she unlocked her apartment door.

"Thanks." Libby readjusted her heavy briefcase and pushed open the door.

"You look like you could use some help." Jessie critically surveyed her friend, taking in her sweat-dampened curls, her pale features and the rumpled blouse that clung to her back.

"What I could use is a long cold drink." Libby flung her briefcase on the sofa and reclaimed her groceries. "I swear I was hallucinating about an icy Coke all the way home. Want one?"

"Sure." Jessie followed her through to the kitchen. "I've been having the same fantasy. The air-conditioning broke down at the courthouse this morning, and I swear it was over a hundred degrees inside."

"It was over a hundred outside!"

"No, just ninety-three," Jessie said seriously.

"Oh, is that all?" Libby laughed. "Why don't you put my groceries away while I pour out two Cokes? You want a piece of that Sacher torte I was making when you were here night before last?"

"Did the icing ever harden?" Jessie asked cautiously.

"No, just dip the cake into it. It tastes great."

"Maybe, but I think it probably loses something in the translation."

"Not in the eating." Libby filled two glasses with ice, added Coke and then handed one to Jessie.

"Make yourself at home. I'll be back in a few minutes. I absolutely have to have a shower."

Five minutes later Libby was beginning to feel human again. The cool water had dissolved the stickiness coating her body. A thin, blue T-shirt clung to her long, slender thighs. She walked back into the living room to find Jessie sitting on the arm of her sofa staring reflectively into space.

"Are you comatose or merely meditating?" Libby picked up the sweating glass of Coke she'd left on the coffee table and took a long satisfying swallow.

"What are you collecting in your study?" Jessie asked.

"Nothing besides dust. Why?"

"Then you have a problem because the dust is organizing."

"What are you raving about?" Libby asked without much real interest. She was hot, tired, and although she refused to acknowledge it, disappointed that there'd been no message from Joe in almost a week.

"I'm not sure. It's about your lump."

Libby frowned curiously and decided to investigate. She paused in the doorway of her tiny study, blinked and looked again. It was still there.

"What the hell is that?" Libby gestured toward the huge shocking-pink shape wedged in between her large oak desk and the wall-to-wall bookcases.

"I asked first." Jessie followed her into the room.

Libby walked over to it and prodded it with an inquiring finger. The material was rough and heavy, but a poke had revealed that it was filled with something very soft. Something . . .

"Oh no!" Libby gasped.

"An inspiration?"

"A premonition," Libby groaned. "Grab one end of that thing and help me drag it out into the living room where I can get a good look at it."

"Personally—" Jessie obligingly took one end "—I've seen all of it that I care to."

"Just pull." Libby tugged it through the door and into the middle of her living room.

Jessie plunked down on the sofa and studied the object over the rim of her glass. "It clashes with the decor," she finally offered. "It also takes up most of your floor space."

"Damn! Do you know what this overgrown monstrosity is?"

"A free-form sculpture? Revenge from a dissatisfied student?"

"Close. It's revenge from a dissatisfied father."

"How do you figure that?"

"Because it wasn't there when I left for work this morning, and the only other person with a key is my father. But he's got the wrong victim. I wasn't the one who asked for it, although I certainly wouldn't have minded the sheets."

"Listening to you is like listening to someone read the dictionary. All the words are familiar, but taken together they don't make any sense."

"It's a mattress. More specifically, a feather mattress."

"A mattress?" Jessie gave it a tentative kick. "Why shocking pink?"

"Who knows." Libby shrugged. "But I have no intention of being stuck with it. This is all Joe's fault."

"He likes shocking-pink mattresses?" Jessie raised an eloquent eyebrow.

"He just likes being difficult. He had this bright idea of throwing in a linen chest as a requirement for the bride."

"And your father's called your bluff!" Jessie chortled.

"It would certainly seem so. Which should also mean that they've returned the contract." And given me an impeccable excuse to call Joe, Libby thought. Her spirits took an unexpected leap, and she hurried into the study to find the contract. Sure enough, it was sitting in the middle of her cluttered desk. Picking it up, she went back into the living room and promptly tripped over the brilliant pink, amorphous blob.

"That's got to go!" she pronounced.

"I agree." Jessie drained the last of her Coke. "The question is to where?"

"Joe put it in the contract. Let him figure out what to do with it."

"Good idea," Jessie approved. "Where do you want to store it until he picks it up?"

"I don't. If that thing is over here, it could be weeks before he gets around to removing it. But if it's in his living room, I guarantee he'll get rid of it at once."

"Clever, but how do you plan on getting it from here to there?"

"Cab." Libby grinned. "Lots of businesses use them to deliver packages."

"That thing is not a package," Jessie declared, stating the obvious.

"A minor detail. Give me a second while I call a cab, and then you can help me maneuver it downstairs."

"Sure, what are friends for?" Jessie said in resignation. "Are you going to call Joe first?"

"Would you admit you were home if you knew someone was bringing you this thing?"

"Good point. Surprise is definitely of the essence. And if he isn't home, make sure no one sees you leaving it on his doorstep or they'll get you for littering. Obscene littering. Go call the cab and let's get this over with."

It wasn't until Libby was wedged into the back seat with the bulging mattress that the very practical consideration of just how she was going to get the thing from the cab up to Joe's apartment occurred to her.

Nervously she chewed her lip as she studied the back of the cab driver's head, wondering if he'd be willing to help. Probably not, she admitted in resignation, remembering how he'd been convulsed with laughter as he'd watched her and Jessie shove it into the back seat. Not only had he not offered any assistance, but he'd demanded a double fare.

Men, Libby thought in disgust as the cab came to a halt in front of Joe's apartment building.

"They expectin' you, honey?" The man brayed with raucous laughter.

Libby gave him a weak smile as she rummaged in her purse for the fare as well as a sizable tip that she hoped would influence him to help her. She popped out of the back seat and watched in dismay as the mattress expanded to fill the space she'd just vacated.

"How are you planning on getting it in there?" The cabbie scratched his balding head as he watched her ineffectual tugging.

"You wouldn't be willing to help, would you?"

"Nope." He shook his head emphatically. "Wasn't part of the deal."

"Where's you basic sense of humanity?" she wailed.

"This is New York City, lady!"

"It feels more like Hades." Libby could feel a thin trickle of sweat running down her spine as she struggled with the unwieldy mattress.

"Get out of the way, lady." The man snorted in disgust. "I guess if I want my cab back I'll have to help you get that thing out. But I'm warning you, I'm not lugging it inside."

"Agreed." Libby was only too happy to accept whatever help was forthcoming. It wasn't much. With a hefty yank from him, the mattress exploded from the cab to land against the cabbie's brawny chest. He glanced from Libby's slight frame to the bulky thing. "You got no muscles."

"I have lots of muscles. They just aren't very well developed."

"Same difference." He shrugged. "Tell you what, lady, you hold out your arms and I'll drape it over you."

"Thanks."

The mattress settled suffocatingly over her body, and she felt prickles along the length of her legs. She'd probably wind up flat on her back with a bad case of heat prostration and an itchy rash, she thought bleakly.

"Where are you?" The cabbie's muffled voice reached her ears.

"Where the hell do you think I am!" Her patience snapped.

"Now, now, lady. All I meant was that your head was covered. You want I should uncover your eyes?"

"Yes, please." Libby forced her voice into even tones and was rewarded for her effort when the cabbie pulled the mattress away from her face. She blew at the sweaty curl that was glued to her damp forehead and gave him a weak thank-you.

"You're welcome," he grunted, and then grinned. "You look ridiculous."

She pretended not to hear him. "Would you mind opening the lobby doors for me?"

"My pleasure." He swung the door open with a flourish.

Libby swept into the building, sighing in pleasure as the chill air cooled her burning skin. She made her awkward way across the lobby, nodded regally at the security guard, who was trying to pretend he hadn't seen her, and stumbled into the waiting elevator, relieved to find it empty. Her relief was short-lived. On the second floor a middle-aged couple got on the elevator.

Libby focused on the control panel and tried to act nonchalant.

Finally the woman was unable to contain her curiosity any longer and she turned to her companion. "Charlie, you're a psychiatrist. What do you think this is all about?" She gestured toward the flushed Libby.

Charlie tore his fascinated gaze away from his contemplation of the elevator's oak paneling, gave Libby a cursory glance and asked condescendingly, "What does that thing represent to you, dear?" He gave her a toothy smile.

"The total incompetence of the psychiatric profession!" Libby snapped, embarrassment and indignation combining into fury."

"Well!" the woman huffed. "He was just trying to help."

The elevator slid to a silent halt and Libby stalked out, trailing her mattress behind her like a robe of state. "Damn fool!" she mumbled.

By the time she reached Joe's door, she was not only physically drained but also thoroughly exasperated. Even the anticipated pleasure of seeing him had dimmed in the light of the knowledge that she had been very ill-advised to rush across town lugging a mattress. And very unlike her. She wasn't an impetuous person. She generally thought a course of action through before she embarked on it. But her involvement with Joe seemed to be changing her normal behavior patterns, and she wasn't sure that it was a change for the better. Frustration lent strength to her hand and she savagely jabbed his doorbell, holding it down.

The door swung open to reveal a casually dressed Joe. He arched a blonde eyebrow and studied her curiously. "What are we celebrating?"

"Your imprudence in asking for a feather mattress." She trudged into the room, shedding the bulky thing as she went.

"That is a feather mattress?" He stared at it.

"That is a feather mattress." Libby sank down onto the leather chair, avoiding the down sofa. At the moment, she never wanted to see another feather as long as she lived.

"Why bring it here?" he queried as he straightened it out in the middle of his living room floor.

"You were the one who asked for it. You can figure out how to get rid of it."

"Sadist." Joe studied it with a jaundiced eye.

"I prefer to think of it as a total lack of masochistic tendencies on my part." She grinned at him. Her spirits were beginning to rise as the strength of his personality revitalized her.

"Have I disturbed you?" she asked belatedly.

"That thing would disturb a corpse. Does its presence mean that the contract came?"

"Yup." She dug it out of her purse and gave it to him.

"Good, we'll go over it tonight."

She let his assumption that she was free stand. Inventing a fictitious date would only serve to deprive her of his company. "You look like you should have used that mattress instead of lugging it across town." The tips of his fingers lightly traced around the damp line of curls glued to her forehead.

Libby shivered as a burning warmth developed in the wake of his touch. A warmth that had nothing to do with the humid heat outside. She seemed to be frozen in her chair as his hand moved down over her cheek and lightly explored the soft pink indentations of her left ear. Her mouth felt dry and her eyes were focused blindly on the broad expanse of pale yellow knit material that covered the flat muscles of his broad chest.

"You're burning up." Joe frowned at her. "How about a cold drink."

"Love one." Her voice had a breathy quality.

"I'll be back in a minute. You stay here. You should have known better than to travel across town wearing a mattress in this heat."

"The subject never came up before," she said waspishly.

"Women!" Joe snorted. "A man would have had better sense."

"Since it was a man who wished it on me in the first place..."

"Well, I got something for you yesterday that should make up for it."

"Oh?" she replied cautiously, watching as he headed toward the kitchen. Had she been on his mind even a fraction as much as he'd been on hers? Probably not, she concluded realistically. Whatever the fascination Joe seemed to hold for her, it was highly unlikely that it was reciprocated. Especially since she wasn't even sure what she was feeling herself or, more pertinently, why. He was handsome, but not overwhelmingly so. His physique was awesome, but she'd never placed that much importance on physical characteristics. He had a razor-sharp mind and possessed an intuitive logic that was all the more impressive for being instinctive, but she'd known a lot of very clever men in her time. His sense of humor appealed to her, but on the other hand a great many of his antiquated ideas on wives and families exasperated her beyond belief. His good points should have been a trade-off with his bad points. But, curiously enough, they weren't. Everything she learned about Joe left her wanting to know more. Each encounter with him left her eager for the next one. It was a strange set of circumstances. One she'd never run across before and she wasn't sure what she should do about it.

Probably nothing. She jumped up, unwilling to probe any deeper into her feelings. Besides, there wasn't any point. Chances were that by the time she finally figured out just what Joe's appeal actually was, she wouldn't feel that way anymore. They were much too divergent for her attraction to deepen into anything else.

Libby wandered over to the mattress, circled it and then plopped down on it, wondering how comfortable it really was. It was vastly overrated, she decided. She could still feel the floor through the stuffing. She wiggled as the heavy ticking billowed around her.

"What are you doing?" Joe's voice startled her. With her head encased in feathers she hadn't heard his light tread across the dense carpeting.

She lifted her head free of the mattress and glanced at him. Her gaze was level with his worn, blue Adidas. Slowly her eyes moved upward over his strongly molded calves, up past his muscular thighs to come to rest with a compulsive fascination on the slight bulge of his masculinity visible through the faded denim of his jeans.

The impact of the package he dropped near her head shook her out of her reverie and she hastily lowered her gaze. What was the matter with her? Staring at him like he was a steak and she was starving. And she wasn't, she insisted. Maybe a little hungry, but hardly starving.

"Well, aren't you going to open it?" He sank down beside her on the mattress.

"Open it?" she repeated as her eyes swung back to his flat stomach. His words ignited an explosion of desire deep within her as she pictured herself slowly, very slowly, sliding open the yellow metal zipper of his jeans.

"Your present," he said impatiently, pointing to the package beside her. "I told you I was going to get it."

"Oh?" Libby looked blankly at the flowered package.

"Are you all right?" He peered into her flushed face. "I think getting that thing over here has fried your brains."

"No, just destroyed my reputation." Libby giggled, remembering the trip up in the elevator. "Although a cold drink would be nice." She stared pointedly at the chilled bottle of beer he was holding.

"Sorry, I meant to get you one, but I forgot when I saw your present." Joe handed her his beer and Libby glanced uncertainly at it. Somehow sharing one bottle seemed very intimate.

"I could get you a Coke, if you'd prefer," he offered.

"This is okay, I just want something wet." She took a gulp of the brew, swallowing the icy liquid gratefully. "Thanks." She handed the bottle back to him, watching as his firm mouth closed over the neck. Her lips tingled as if they were actually experiencing the pressure and she hastily ducked her head, turning her attention to the package.

Ripping it open, she picked up the plastic-wrapped kit and stared blankly at the brilliant splash of color the red embroidery thread made on the white linen.

"What is it?"

"A picnic cloth for you to embroider . . . for your dowry." He looked immensely pleased with himself. "I wasn't having any luck finding one until Agnes remembered this company in Iowa that did some embroidery for us last year."

"Agnes?" Libby latched on to the name.

"My secretary. Anyway she called them up and they sent us one Federal Express." He sank down beside her.

"You shouldn't have gone to the trouble," she said with absolute sincerity.

"Nonsense, glad to help."

Much more of his help and she'd be a nervous wreck, she thought sourly. First, he landed her with a pink elephant of a feather mattress and then he gave her a project that, if she did it, would keep her busy until her fortieth birthday.

She peered at him from under her lashes, wondering if he was mocking her complete lack of interest in accumulating a hope chest. There was a pleased expression on his face. Deciding that this wasn't the time to probe beneath the surface, Libby tossed the kit on the floor.

"Want any more?" He offered her another drink and, when she shook her head, he drained the last of the beer, set the empty bottle on the coffee table and lay back on the mattress.

"This isn't quite the way I remembered it." He frowned.

"The past has a way of being like that. What I'm curious about is how your grandmother managed to avoid suffocating in the summer. Even with your air-conditioning, this thing is hot. Can you imagine what it would be like if the temperature were in the eighties?"

"But think of the winters. It's like sleeping in a triple thick comforter."

"You could get the same effect in a half-filled water bed," Libby pointed out.

"No, I couldn't. Water beds aren't allowed this high up."

"Don't be picky."

"Lie down beside me and let's see how comfortable this is."

Libby knew it was a bad idea, but two things compelled her to obey. First, it was unthinkable that she give him the impression that she was afraid of close contact with him. And second, quite simply, she wanted to lie beside him and wasn't able to resist the temptation. Cautiously she stretched out beside him.

"Mmm." Joe inched closer to her, causing her muscles to tighten as they made contact with the hard length of him. "It lacks something."

"Oh?" Her concentration was focused on the heat emanating from his body, which was seeping through her denim-clad leg to warm the skin below. Her bare arm was pressed into his muscular chest, and she could feel the hard lines of his rib cage through his knit shirt. Nervously she licked her lips as a shiver chased over her skin.

"Maybe it works better in a different positon." His words drifted through her mind. She was too busy dealing with the reality of his touch to try to follow a conversation. So she was taken by surprise when his muscular arms encircled her slight frame, turning her onto her side and fitting her back into his chest.

"What are you doing?" she demanded.

"Trying to find a comfortable position." He sighed. "But it's not easy." He shifted restlessly, managing to cover her small breast with one large hand as he did so.

Libby wiggled her trim hips against his hard abdomen, her breath catching as she felt his burgeoning manhood burning its imprint into her softness.

"Joe . . ." she began uncertainly.

"Shh." He tucked her head under his chin and pulled her back against him. "We're testing the mattress."

No, she mentally corrected him. What they were testing were the limits of her endurance. She closed her eyes and relaxed into him. The pressure of his body down her back brought her skin to tingling life and she absorbed the sensation, letting his warmth feed the passion beginning to quicken deep within her. His left hand suddenly slipped under her T-shirt. She instinctively sucked in her breath as his large hand splayed across her rib cage, expelling air on a shaky sigh while her mind concentrated on the feel of his long fingers searing into her quivering skin. His blunt fingertips were barely brushing against the soft swell of her left breast and time seemed suspended as she waited. Her eyes slid shut as she clenched her teeth and willed him to move.

The buzzing in her ears released her from her suspended state and she gulped in air. Promptly forgetting to expel it when his hand slowly slipped around her back to release the clasp on her bra. Her flash of awareness at the expertise with which he accomplished it was drowned by the flood of anticipation that inundated her as he flicked the lacy scrap aside.

She shuddered as his roughened fingers trailed over her back. The passion building in her flared as his hands covered her bare breasts. For several seconds he was still, allowing the warmth of his hands to permeate her breasts, making them swell with anticipation. A quiver quickened to life deep in the heart of her femininity as he slowly began to rotate his palms over the velvety mounds of flesh, causing the tips to harden with aching desire. A tremor shook her slight limbs as he gently tugged the turgid peak between his thumb and forefinger.

A sobbing moan escaped through her clenched teeth, and she wiggled deeper into his hold, glorying in the state of his arousal. Slowly his left hand trailed tantalizingly down her rib cage, pausing at the waistband of her jeans to dip his forefinger into her navel.

Libby shifted restlessly and opened her mouth, but no words escaped. What was there to say? She didn't have to tell him how what he was doing was effecting her. He could feel that himself. And she didn't want to tell him to stop. Not quite yet. Soon she would. Soon she lost her train of thought as his wandering hand suddenly lowered her zipper and slipped inside her jeans.

Her abdomen fluttered frantically as his fingers splayed possessively over it, and her breath escaped in short gasps as she began to shiver uncontrollably. She twisted as his hand suddenly slipped lower.

"Joe!" she began to protest, but the passion coloring her voice gave lie to her objections.

"It's all right, my exquisite Libby." He moved, rolling her on her back and looming above her.

"You shouldn't . . . I want . . ."

"Whatever you want." His husky voice stoked her bubbling passion as he slowly removed his hand, trailing his fingers lightly over her heated femininity. "You're so perfect," he praised. "I won't do anything you don't like."

"That's not the trouble. The trouble is that I like it all too well. I should . . ."

She gasped as his warm mouth closed over the distended peak of one taut breast. A piercing shaft of sweetness zig-zagged through her as his devouring mouth melted away her resistance. Her fingers grasped his hair, threading through the silken strands and holding his head tightly against her.

"Not here on the floor. Not with you," Joe murmured, suddenly levering himself upward. Before she could react, he picked her up, cradling her possessively against his broad chest. "We'll use my bedroom." He strode toward the hall-way.

Said the spider to the fly flashed through her mind, but she banished the thought. She tucked her head into his neck, shivering at the prickly feel of his hair-roughened jaw scraping over her soft cheek. She didn't want to look in his eyes. She was afraid of what she might find. She didn't even want to think. She wanted to feel. She was an adult woman, old enough to take what she wanted. Old enough to take the consequences of her actions; that corollary chased through her mind, but she ignored it. Life was for the living, and right this minute she intended to live.

8

A DREAMY SMILE curved Libby's slightly swollen lips, and she sleepily stretched her limbs in almost feline satisfaction. A satisfaction that was abruptly shattered as her foot encountered the rough warmth of a hair-covered leg.

Her eyes flew open in shock, and she found herself staring at the magnificent lines of Joe's relaxed body. A burning warmth engulfed her as memory came flooding back, bringing all her doubts with it. Her eyes flew to his face, and she relaxed infinitesimally as she realized that he had not yet surfaced from the sleep that had overtaken both of them after the cataclysmic climax of their passion.

Hungrily she traced the sleep-softened lines of his face, which were barely visible in the dim glow of twilight. Her gaze slipped over the glimmering gold of his hair-covered chest, compulsively following the line that arrowed down over his abdomen. Her breath caught in her lungs, and she touched the tip of her tongue to the center of her upper lip as an ember of lingering desire blazed to life deep within her. A spark she quickly extinguished. That was how she'd wound up in his bed, listening to her emotions and ignoring what her reason was trying to tell her. But even the sure knowledge that their lovemaking had been a mistake couldn't make her regret it.

Euphoria momentarily washed over her. It had been an incredible experience, a revelation. Lovemaking, as Joe defined it, had a depth and a width of emotion that had taken her by surprise. In his arms she'd lost all her inhibitions. She'd become a warm, sensual woman, eagerly taking all that he gave and returning it tenfold. For the first time in her life, she truly understood why people were willing to risk everything for a lover. But even so, going to bed with him had been a bad idea; she was certain.

At best, their lovemaking had come too soon. There were too many unanswered questions floating around her mind about him. Too many niggling little uncertainties that made it impossible for her to accurately predict what his attitude toward her would be now that she'd committed the monumental indiscretion of going to bed with him. A disturbing echo of his comment that Myrna wasn't the type of woman one married returned to haunt her. Why wasn't Myrna the type of woman one married? Was it because she had allowed him to make love to her outside the sanctity of marriage? Could he really be that hypocritical?

It was possible. Libby answered her own question with a growing feeling of unease. It all depended on just how much of his father's old-world values he'd absorbed.

As illogical as it was, given that marriage was not an issue, Libby wanted him to think well of her. To respect her as a woman in her own right. She liked Joe. And more importantly, she respected him. Joe Landowski had a deeply held core of religious and philosophical beliefs, unlike so many of the men she knew who believed in nothing they couldn't see or touch. He was strong and not just physically. Her eyes strayed down the firm lines of his body as he sprawled across two-thirds of the king-size bed. Yes, there was a lot she liked about him.

And a lot she didn't like. She forced herself to face reality. A reality that hadn't changed simply because she'd just shared the most cataclysmic event of her life with him. A lot of his ideas about the proper role of a wife were straight out of *The Male Chauvinist's Handbook*.

So what did it all add up to, she wondered tiredly. Jo
seemed like a kaleidoscope. Shifting and changing pattern
while she watched. Revealing and concealing titillating
glimpses of his personality. All of which made it almost im
possible for her to predict his reaction to her having allowed
him to make love to her. Would he consign her to the same
limbo as Myrna?

Her answer came almost immediately. The even cadence
of his breathing changed and he stretched, his slightly abrasive leg moving over her much softer one. But Libby barely
noticed, waiting nervously as he opened his eyes. They were
warm with a residual glow of sexual satisfaction and, as she
watched, a knowing gleam brightened them.

"Why didn't you waken me, my lovely?" He gently
squeezed her hand. Nervously she scooted out of reach. She
wasn't certain what was the right thing to do, but she most
definitely knew what was the wrong and that was to let him
touch her. Once he held her close to him, she'd forget everything but her desire to touch him. "Libby?" He shook his head
as if scattering the last remnants of sleep and then propped
himself up on his elbow. "What's wrong? You must know
that—"

"I'd like to take a shower," she hastily interrupted. She
didn't care if she was acting like a blithering idiot instead of
the mature woman that she knew herself to be. She didn't
want to know what he thought about what had just happened. Later, when she felt more in control of her skittering
emotions she'd listen. But for now she desperately needed
breathing space, to be away from the magnetism of his physical presence, to get her off-center world back into perspective.

"Libby, we—"

"And I'm starved," she said brightly, inwardly wincing at
the high pitch of her tone. She tumbled off the bed and be-

gan to pick up her clothes from the floor where she'd hastily discarded them.

"All right." The calm normalcy of his voice helped to still her quivering nerves. "Go take your shower and I'll see what's in the refrigerator. Then we can tackle the latest version of the contract."

"Fine." She escaped into the luxurious master bath.

Thirty minutes later, replete on the remains of a bacon quiche and leftover steak, Libby picked the contract up off the floor, skirted the pink mattress and sank down on the sofa, tucking her feet up under her. Comfortable as the mattress was for sitting, she had no intention of using it. If she did, Joe might think that she was angling for more of his lovemaking and, while the idea held a certain appeal, she knew she didn't dare risk it. Not while she hadn't as yet come to terms with what had already happened. All she had managed to do so far was relegate it to the back of her mind, to be examined later without the distracting influence of Joe's presence.

She watched as he picked up the mattress and dropped it over a chair.

"How on earth are you going to get rid of that?"

"I think I'll keep it."

"Keep it?"

"Uh-huh. I'll give it to my father for a Christmas present."

"I'll help you wrap it." She laughed and then abruptly sobered. Christmas was six months away. Who knew if they'd even be talking by then?

To her relief, he seemed to see nothing wrong with her offer. He picked up the embroidery kit that she'd left on the floor and handed it to her.

"Why don't you start on this while I write on the contract?"

Libby eyed the kit with distaste. "Because first of all it's my contract to write on and, secondly, there's at least a thousand hours work in that thing."

"Well, if you start now, there'll only be nine hundred ninety-nine left."

"Somehow I don't find much comfort in that thought."

"Every great journey starts with a single step."

"And every would-be philosopher starts with a few trite sayings." Depositing the kit back on the floor, she picked up the contract.

"At the rate you're going, it's going to be winter before you get that picnic cloth done!"

"Or the year 2000. Now let me see." She studied the first page.

"We've got the mattress, so you can simply initial that to show that that's been taken care of," she suggested.

"*You've* got the mattress," Libby corrected, obediently initialing it. "I still would have preferred the twelve sets of sheets."

"Maybe," he sounded doubtful, "but considering what the mattress looks like, I rather doubt that you'd have cared for any sheets our fathers would have turned up with."

"That's true," she conceded.

"And I got you the picnic cloth. All you have to do is embroider it."

"In my copious free time!"

"If you were willing to stay at home, you'd have lots of free time."

"Now then," she began, ignoring him, "let's see what else we've got. We're in agreement that we'll live in New York City, right?"

"Yes," he replied, nodding.

"That basically leaves the kids and my job."

"The six kids." He propped his feet up on the antique ceramic tiles inlaid in the top of his coffee table.

"Joe, be reasonable," Libby moaned. "It's immoral to do more than simply replace ourselves in this crowded world."

"With your genetic background it's quite possible we'd turn out a son who was capable of making a tremendous contribution to mankind. Would you deny his gifts to the world?"

"Or hers! Girls can make just as big a contribution as men, and, anyway, that's grossly illogical. If you follow that train of thought, I should have a dozen kids."

"I'm willing." His eyes took on a brilliant gleam, and she knew he was remembering what had happened earlier. Her stomach twisted with pleasure at the memory, but she refused to allow it to influence her. This might only be pretend—even if they did seem to consistently forget the fact—but she still refused to deviate from what she believed in.

"I'm not even sure I like kids," she admitted reluctantly, worried that the admission might lower her value in Joe's eyes. He seemed to have the harebrained notion that all women loved children indiscriminately.

"What's not to like?"

Libby stared at him. "Well, for starters, there's dirty diapers, irrational crying, around the clock eating..."

"Ah, come on. It's not that bad," he chided. "I'm willing to give it the two-o'clock feeding. I suppose one bottle a day won't hurt."

"You're planning on starving it the rest of the time?"

"I said one bottle a day. Naturally you'll breast-feed the children."

"There's no 'naturally' about it," Libby sputtered.

"But it's best for the baby as well as the mother. It returns your internal parts to a prepregnancy state much quicker."

"So I can get pregnant again?" she queried sourly.

"Women nursing and not using birth control have children spaced eighteen months apart, whereas nonnursing mothers have them twelve months apart."

"What a comfort!" Libby snorted. "Anyone with a new baby who doesn't practice some form of birth control deserves a kid every year. I have no intention of nursing."

"We'll see," he soothed.

"Nursing ties you down. My poor cousin couldn't be gone for longer than two hours until her kids were almost eight months old. They refused to accept a bottle."

"You could try, and if you didn't like it, you could switch to a bottle."

"And no hassle?" She eyed him narrowly, not trusting his offer. It sounded too much like capitulation.

"No hassle." He spread his large hands. "If you honestly don't like nursing, you aren't going to be doing yourself or the baby any good."

"Oh." She was rather taken aback by what he'd said. He was absolutely right, but she'd never have expected him to admit it to himself, let alone to her. Well, nursing's solved." She scribbled in the margin.

"But that doesn't solve the underlying problem," she pointed out. "I'm still not sure I like children. I certainly don't care for them in general. I feel nothing but exasperation when my friends' kids do supposedly cute things that seem to amuse their parents no end."

"What about those kids you're bringing over next week?"

"My cousin's boys." Libby frowned. "Well, I like them. Mostly," she amended, shuddering slightly as she remembered a few times when she most definitely hadn't liked them. "But I've never had them longer than a weekend. I've always been able to give them back before they became a nuisance. But you don't get return privileges with your own."

"You won't want to," Joe predicted confidently. "You'll love your own six, wait and see."

"Two, I'll compromise at two." She said firmly, writing that down.

"What if they're both girls?" he demanded.

"Oh, no you don't! That's how we got from one to two in the first place."

"Whatever works." He chuckled while she continued down the page.

"Hmm, we agreed on their religion, but got hung up on education."

"You got hung up," Joe corrected. "I knew what I wanted."

"Whether it's right or not," she countered.

"It's important to reinforce values taught at home," he said, repeating his earlier argument. Especially with teenagers who are already suffering the strains of adolescence."

"You have a point, but you can't generalize about kids on the basis of a few. We might have a gifted child who would benefit from a specialized school."

"Perhaps," he conceded. "How about if we agree to Catholic schools through high school, and we'll consider letting them go to a secular college if there's a good reason."

"Through grammar school, then we discuss what high school they want to attend with them and leave the choice of a college entirely up to them. By the time they're old enough to go away to college, they're old enough to make their own decisions."

"When they pay their own bills, then they make their own decisions."

"Money is irrelevant."

"Only if you've got plenty."

"I refuse to use money as a weapon."

"I wasn't asking you to. I will," he goaded.

"No!" Libby snapped, furiously writing. "Only up to grammar school."

"But—"

"It's my turn at the contract," she emphatically reminded him. "Which only leaves one area: my job."

"Tell you what." Joe leaned back and stared at the ceiling. "If you want a job, I'll pay you to be a wife and mother."

"No! I'm a highly skilled professional. I don't need some overbearing man to patronize me."

He began to voice a mild protest, "I just thought—"

"No, you didn't. You didn't think at all, and you also aren't paying attention. I told you that the money isn't the crux of it. It's the job satisfaction I get from teaching and research. You can't replace that with money."

"Try replacing it with kids."

"You aren't listening to a word I'm saying!" she shouted. "You . . ." She paused, and taking a deep breath made an almost visible effort to get a grip on herself. She was normally a very even-tempered person who responded to a difference of opinion with logic and reason. She'd never had anything but faint contempt for people who couldn't argue a point without yelling, but Joe didn't respond to either logic or reason. Or anything else that a rational individual might say. She glanced at his implacable face. Arguing with him wasn't an exercise in logic. It was an exercise in futility. But she wasn't going to allow him to maneuver her into acting like a stereotype of a shrewish woman.

"Raising kids isn't the same thing at all. It may have it's rewards, although I'm going to reserve judgment on that, but they aren't the same. Or even comparable." So far, so good. She silently congratulated herself on the calm reasonableness of her voice. Encouraged, she continued.

"I don't begin to understand your fascination with the dubious joys of big business, but I haven't asked you to give it up and stay at home with a family. Even though it's you who wants all those kids!" She was unable to resist the dig.

"That's not the same thing at all." He gave her a superior smile that raised her blood pressure twenty points.

"Oh?" She glared at him.

"But we've already settled that."

"Oh, no we haven't! All we've settled is that you made more money than I did."

"Lots more money."

"And all that proves—" her voice rose with the strength of her feelings "—is that society has some very cockeyed notions on the worth of the various professions."

"Shame on you, Liberty Joy Michalowski." His face assumed a shocked expression that didn't quite camouflage the gleam of laughter deep in his bright blue eyes. "Blaming your shortcomings on society."

"My shortcomings?" she sputtered. "We were talking about money."

"Or your lack thereof."

"Quit trying to change the subject! We were talking about my job."

"And how poorly paid it was."

"It isn't poorly paid!" she insisted, completely losing her temper. At least, it isn't by any standards except those of a . . . a . . ." She ground to a frustrated stop.

"Exploitative capitalistic pig?" he suggested innocently.

"That does it!" She slammed her coffee cup down on the lamp table and jumped up, absolutely furious. "I don't know why I bother. You don't want to discuss anything. All you want to do is mock what I'm trying to say. You aren't looking for a compromise!" she yelled into his startled face. "You want capitulation and you can damn well find it somewhere else!" She grabbed her purse and ran out of the apartment, ignoring his surprised expletive.

Who cared what he thought, she fumed. Too enraged to wait for the elevator, she plunged into the stairwell and ran down the eleven flights of stairs, emerged into the lobby and cannoned into Joe's waiting arms.

She stepped backward, looked down her nose at him, and with a haughty sniff, stalked across the lobby, ignoring the security guard who was watching curiously.

"Libby, listen to me." He matched his pace to hers.

She lifted her chin and ignored him. She was almost to the exit when Joe's large hand closed around her upper arm and he yanked her toward a set of doors to their extreme left.

"What do you think you're doing?" She glared pointedly at his hand curled around her arm.

"The garage is in the basement, through these doors."

"So what? I came in a taxi. With your mattress!"

"Don't drag past grievances into a fight," he said calmly.

"All right," she snipped. "I imagine with your attitude you've lots of experience in the proper way to conduct a fight. Unfortunately, since I normally deal with rational men . . ."

"Rational, hell! They must be dead if they can take your attitude in silence." He maneuvered her through the doorway.

"I told you—"

"And I'm telling you—" his voice was steely "—that I'm not leaving you to wander around New York City after dark in a snit."

"Snit!"

"Childish snit." He hustled her down a flight of stairs and through the garage.

"I don't have snits."

"No?" He gave her a sardonic glance. "Then you're giving a damn good imitation of one."

"I am angry!" She spat at him. "Furiously angry at your obstinate, bullheaded refusal to face facts."

"Strange how an intellectual type like you should lose her cool at the first hint of opposition while a poor businessman like me manages to maintain a calm perspective."

"That's because you're so armored in your own chauvinism that you don't even know how annoying you are."

"Keep telling yourself that if it makes you feel any better." He bundled her into his car.

It didn't make her feel any better. She hurriedly buckled the shoulder harness while he slipped into the driver's seat. As volatile as her emotions were right now, she didn't want him to touch her. Who knew what might happen?

Libby leaned back against the soft leather seat and closed her eyes to discourage any more comments from Joe. Nonetheless, she was unable to entirely suppress the slight feeling of pique that he didn't even try to talk to her. He seemed perfectly content to ignore her as he steered the car with mathematical precision through the heavy city traffic.

By the time he'd double-parked in front of her apartment building, her uncharacteristic anger had faded, leaving confusion in its wake. She released her seat belt and glanced uncertainly at him. He was watching the traffic through his sideview mirror. It was obvious that he didn't intend to come up with her. Not that she'd been going to invite him in, she thought on a residual spark of anger. She released the catch and swung open the door, hesitating a brief second.

"Good night," she finally said, jumping out of the car and slamming the door shut behind her.

He made no response, merely waiting until she was inside the building before pulling away and disappearing into traffic.

Libby let herself into her apartment, trying to keep her mind a blank, but it proved an impossibility. The empty space in her living room where the hideous pink mattress had laid brought the evening's events rushing back.

She wandered over to the liquor cabinet and poured herself a glass of Scotch, then wandered out to the kitchen to find some ice. The pristine state of her countertops reminded her of an earlier grievance, and she hurried back to the living room. Taking the contract out of her purse, she hastily scrawled in a demand that Joe clean up after himself. "There." She tossed it down on the coffee table.

"Aggravating man!" She took a swallow of the amber liquid, not even noticing when it burned a path to her stomach. She winced as she caught sight of herself in the mirror over the stereo. There was a wild glint in her eyes and her hair was a tumbled mess.

"What is the matter with me?" she demanded of herself, sinking down into a chair. She closed her eyes and slowly counted to ten. It didn't help. Her thoughts still raced like a forty-five record being played at seventy-eight. But why? Why had she allowed Joe to shake her out of her calm, intellectual approach to life? When all was said and done, they were merely playing a game.

Libby sighed, no longer able to keep at bay what was really bothering her. What had really set her nerves on end and triggered her violent response to Joe's teasing. A tremulous sigh shook her as her mind began to slowly replay the sequence of his lovemaking. Her face softened into dreamy lines and she wiggled deeper into her sofa as a glowing warmth began to grow in her abdomen. Determinedly she turned off her memories.

What had begun as a relatively simple conspiracy to get their parents off their backs had suddenly taken on unexpected dimensions. "Thanks to you." Libby placed the blame squarely on her own shoulders. "You were so eager to see him that you didn't stop to think. You lugged that blessed mattress across town and burst in on him." With the advantage of hindsight, she knew that she should have waited. Waited until she was more in control of her emotions. But when would that have been, she thought wryly. She'd been off balance since the first moment she'd met Joe.

"Oh hell," she muttered despairingly. What had happened to her well-ordered life, and more importantly, where did they go from here?

After her outburst Joe would probably decide that she represented more trouble than his father did. And, even if he wanted to continue the negotiations, how should she treat him? The free and easy camaraderie that had developed between them during the past few weeks had been swallowed

up in the conflagration of their sexual encounter. At least on
her part. She frowned thoughtfully as she realized that he
hadn't been as emotionally involved in their argument as
she'd been. As a matter of fact, he'd seemed more amused
than angry. Did he find her humorous? The appalling thought
chilled her. It was possible, she admitted. Her knowledge of
lovemaking had been infinitesimal beside the expertise he'd
shown. An expertise that had elicited a headlong sensual response she had made no attempt to disguise. Perhaps he had
found her limited experience unsatisfying. Or even worse,
pathetically inept; the terrible thought refused to be banished.

"Stop it, Liberty Joy Michalowski," she ordered aloud.
Trying to second-guess a rational individual was risky, let
alone one with Joe's convoluted thought processes. Her eyes
strayed to the phone, but she hastily slammed the lid down
on the fugitive impulse. She would not call him. She might
not be sure of much in this unprecedented situation she found
herself in, but she did know that calling him without an air-
tight excuse was a bad idea.

A sudden feeling of uncertainty shook her as she remembered that Joe was supposed to be playing mother to her four
young cousins Tuesday. She wondered if that was still on. He
hadn't canceled, but then it might have slipped his mind in
the light of what else had happened. She'd forgotten all about
it, and not only were they her cousins, but it had also been
her idea. This definitely represented a reason for calling him.
She brightened at the thought. But not tonight. That might
smack too much of a desperate attempt to make amends and
she had more pride than that.

Besides, she wasn't the least bit sorry for what she'd said,
merely for the emotional, illogical way she'd said it. She
should have been calm and judicious instead of screaming at
him like a fishwife. She winced as an echo of her anger-

charged voice filtered through her mind. There was something about Joe Landowski that could shake her out of the calm of thirty years.

9

MONDAY NIGHT FOUND LIBBY comfortably sprawled on her living room floor in front of an air-conditioning vent, trying to formulate a casual way of asking Joe if he was still interested in playing mother to her cousins tomorrow. It was turning out to be a lot harder than she'd originally thought. Every opening sentence that she'd tried out in her mind either sounded incredibly insecure or falsely hearty.

"You have to do something." She addressed the ceiling and then rolled over onto her stomach to stare at the legs on her couch. She was supposed to pick up the boys before breakfast tomorrow. If Joe were pulling out, she had to tell Elizabeth this evening.

"Blast!" She flipped over, jackknifed up, wrapped her arms around her legs and dropped her chin on her jean-clad knee. Dithering indecision was a totally unexpected state for her and she didn't like it at all. She was used to being well in control of both herself and events. All this floundering around, trying to decide how to approach him, was exasperating, but she didn't seem to be able to help herself. She had barely managed to stifle her initial impulse to call him up and apologize for the temper tantrum she'd indulged in last Thursday.

Libby covered her eyes with her arm. A definite mistake as slowly, tantalizingly, her mind began to replay what had happened last week in Joe's bedroom. She snapped open her eyes in repudiation of the memories. That was what was really bothering her, she admitted honestly. Not knowing how their having made love was going to change things between them. She released her breath on a long shaky sigh. That's what had unnerved her to the extent that she'd vented her feelings of doubt and uncertainty by screaming at the author of those doubts.

She worried that Joe's silence was telling her what he thought. It had been four days since their fight and she hadn't heard a word from him. Not one. That could mean he'd decided to forget both her and the negotiations.

But not necessarily, she tried to encourage herself. Four days wasn't all that long. And, besides, she suddenly remembered, he'd already mentioned that he was working long hours trying to straighten out a design problem. His silence probably had nothing to do with the fact that they were now lovers. If they actually were lovers. Libby thoughtfully chewed her lower lip. What exactly made a man and a woman lovers? Simply going to bed together?

But she and Joe had more than that in common. They shared the same sense of humor, the same ethnic and religious background and an appreciation of each other's minds. At least she respected his, she thought grimly. Heaven only knew what Joe thought of her own capabilities. They also shared a predilection for Charlie Chaplin movies and Agatha Christie mysteries. Did all that make them lovers?

"Oh hell!" She jumped to her feet and glared at the phone sitting on the table. She had to do something. Something beside dither, she told herself scathingly.

Taking a deep breath, Libby started toward the phone, coming to a surprised halt as it suddenly rang. Her heart stopped and then began to race. Nervous, she wiped damp palms over her denim-clad thighs. It was Joe. A sense of foreboding filled her. She knew it. He was calling to tell her that he'd changed his mind about having the boys tomorrow.

"It's probably someone selling something." She chastised herself, grabbing the phone.

"Hello," she said, and almost dropped it when Joe's deep voice answered her. Oh, Lord, it really was him. Her stomach cramped nervously.

"Libby, are you there?" His impatient voice shook her out of her reverie.

"Of course, I'm here. What did you want?" She decided to ignore the social pleasantries in favor of getting to the heart of the matter. If she was about to go the way of the late, unlamented Myrna, she'd just as soon know it at once.

"To show you something."

"Over the phone?" She teased as a surge of pure relief welled through her. He wasn't about to terminate their association. He was behaving normally. At least normally for him. For anyone else, that kind of behavior would come under a variety of headings, none of which could possibly be labeled normal.

"Don't be any more difficult than you can help. I'll be there in twenty minutes." He abruptly hung up, leaving Libby staring at the dead receiver in her hand. So her outburst of last Thursday was not to be mentioned, she mused. Which was fine with her. She was perfectly willing to consign it to oblivion. But he'd also made no reference to what else had happened. Were they also to ignore that? Did that mean he wanted to forget it?

Slowly she hung up. Not necessarily, she tried to reassure herself. First of all, from what she'd heard, men weren't as inclined to discuss their feelings as women. And, second, she *had* cut him off when he'd tried to say something when they'd still been in bed together. So it was hardly any wonder that he'd slipped back into his normal mode of behavior.

She wondered curiously what he could want to show her. Something their fathers had delivered maybe. Whatever it was it couldn't possibly top a shocking-pink feather mattress. Feeling incredibly lighthearted, she hurried into the kitchen to make coffee and hide the remains of the boxed cake

with its canned icing that she'd made yesterday in a fit of re-
bellion.

Not quite fifteen minutes later, she was opening the door
for him. He certainly hadn't wasted any time getting there.

"Ready?" He glanced with resignation at her jeans, but to
her surprise he refrained from commenting on them.

"For what?" she asked cautiously, glancing past his empty
arms into the hallway behind him.

"I said I had something to show you."

"So show me."

"It's not here. Come on. My car's in the parking lot under
this building. Someone was already double-parked out
front."

"Some people have no respect for the law." Libby giggled
as she grabbed her purse from the table beside the door and
then double-checked the lock before she allowed him to hurry
her down the hallway.

The feel of his large hand curled around the soft skin of her
upper arm was doing strange things to her equilibrium. The
warmth of his fingers permeated her skin and zinged along
her nerve endings. Her reaction to his touch seemed more
pronounced than it had ever been, she realized with a sinking feeling. Almost as if what they'd shared last Thursday had
made her more receptive to him. As if he'd fine-tuned her
body to receive the sensitive vibrations he was sending out.
It was a disquieting thought.

Libby forcibly banished the idea as they walked through
the dimly lit underground lot. This was the first time she'd
seen him in days—four long days—and she intended to make
the most of her time with him. Not waste it in an orgy of introspection. He helped her into his Ferrari and she watched
as he rounded the silver hood, his large body moving with
an exquisite coordination that seemed almost feline. Like a
tiger. She half closed her eyes as she remembered his muscles

rippling beneath his bare skin when he was poised above her last week.

A fluttery feeling began to grow deep in her abdomen and her breathing shortened. The lemony scent of his after-shave drifted across the front seat as he slid into the car and she took a deep breath, allowing the fragrance to penetrate her mind.

" . . . law, to say nothing of common sense." The last part of his sentence penetrated the sensual fog that had engulfed her.

"What?" She blinked at him.

"I was talking about your seat belt. You have to wear it." He reached across her and pulled out the harness. "Just a second. It's twisted."

"I can..." She shrank back into the gray glove-leather seat as he began to fiddle with the strap. His thigh was pressed tightly against hers, and even through two layers of denim she could feel the warmth of his skin. She shifted and his forearm made contact with her shoulder, bringing it to shivering life and making her yearn for something more intimate. Her eyes slid shut as the heat from his large frame engulfed her like a cloud. A sensually charged cloud that made her skin tingle.

"There." The click of the seat belt sounded loudly in the enclosed car. Joe moved slightly and his hard chest was suddenly pressed against her soft breasts.

She gasped and her breath became suspended in her lungs. She held herself immobile, savoring the exquisite feel of his muscles bearing down on her.

"Is it all right?" she asked inanely.

"Most definitely." His lips began to nuzzle the soft skin under her ear.

Libby shuddered as the slightly raspy texture of his jaw scraped over the tender surface of her neck. The abrasive quality of his caress was unbearably exciting and she allowed her body to melt into him, making no attempt to remain aloof. She craved contact with him and she saw no reason to deny herself.

"Hmm, you taste delicious. Like a fresh nectarine tart with globs of whipped cream," he murmured softly as his teeth lightly nibbled at her earlobe. A series of tremors shook her and she arched her head back, encouraging his wandering lips. Her hands slid over his muscular forearms, over the bulge of his massive biceps and up over his shoulders. Her fingertips burned as they caressed the supple skin of his corded neck and then slipped up to become entangled in the silken strands of his hair.

His wandering lips left her neck and began to place teasing kisses at the corner of her mouth.

"Don't." Libby shifted restlessly beneath the force of the emotion tearing through her.

"Don't?" Joe mused. "What do you want? This, perhaps?" His hand suddenly slipped beneath her camisole top to close over her bare breast.

"Yes!" she gasped, not even attempting to deny the effect he was having on her. It would have been useless anyway, she thought fatalistically. He could feel the hardening bud of her breast against his slightly callused palm.

As if to reward her for her honesty, his parted lips came down over her mouth and his tongue plunged inside.

She shuddered at the delicious intrusion and her fingers clenched in his hair. Then his devouring mouth forced her head backward, and her lips opened wider.

Libby gasped, inhaling the warmth of his breath. It flowed to her lungs, clinging to her senses like honey. She wiggled frantically as his caressing hand suddenly caught the hard tip of her breast between his thumb and forefinger and began to gently tug the turgid flesh. The awesome flood of passion inundating her wiped out such elemental considerations as the fact that she was seated in the front seat of a car. The only thing she was certain of was that she craved the feel of his bare flesh against hers. With a moan of frustrated desire, which was swallowed up by his demanding mouth, she arched into him. Unfortunately her movement caught the gearshift lever, nudging it into neutral.

"Damn!" Joe jerked upward as the car began to roll. He hit the brake and repositioned the gear.

Libby was much slower to surface. She blinked, trying to bring the leather dashboard into focus. Her lips felt swollen and her whole body pulsated with frustrated desire. A state she tried to hide in light of Joe's rapid recovery.

"Bucket seats are not conducive to kissing." He smiled tenderly at her.

Libby grinned back weakly and watched in bemusement as he leaned toward her. His golden head suddenly swooped, and he planted a burning kiss on the dusky-pink tip of her breast. Her exposed breast. That she'd not even realized her shirt had been pulled up registered briefly before the burning warmth of his mouth shot through her.

Slowly, seemingly reluctantly, he withdrew and he tenderly pulled her top down over her throbbing flesh. "First things first," he said softly. "You're distracting enough when I'm dealing with your mind, let alone with your body."

She was distracting! He would probably register on the Richter scale!

"Libby..." He gave her a strangely uncertain look. "About last Friday..."

"I think the less said about that the better," she hurriedly inserted, loath to spoil their evening by dredging up a past argument.

"I agree, but before we consign it to the past, I want you to know that I wasn't intentionally trying to make you angry. I didn't realize you were serious until you lost your temper."

"It's okay. Now where are we going?" She determinedly changed the subject.

"Wait and be surprised," he said, turning his attention back to the road.

Libby took advantage of the drive to calm her jangled nerves. The early-evening traffic was heavy, and it wasn't until they were on Thirty-eighth Street, east of Park Avenue, that she realized Joe was not taking her back to his apartment. Just as she was about to ask where they were going, he pulled into the curb beside a small park sitting like a dark green jewel in the hot city.

"How beautiful." She watched a toddler playing on the grass under the watchful eyes of a neatly uniformed, middle-aged woman. A nanny, Libby surmised. She certainly fit in with the neighborhood. Libby glanced at the gorgeous old town houses rimming the park. The whole area was redolent of good taste and the means to indulge it. It was an area of New York City she'd never seen before.

"Definitely," he murmured, his bright blue gaze fastened on her face.

"Where are we?" She pretended not to catch his double entendre and hastily climbed out of the car before he could help her. It had taken her most of the drive to return to some semblance of normalcy and she didn't want to risk touching him yet.

"Murray Hill." He pointed toward a large corner house directly across from them. "That's what I brought you to see."

"The red brick?" She studied it curiously. It was huge. Two full stories with a dormered attic. A broad step led up to the shining black door with a gleaming brass knocker. There were six windows set approximately three feet apart to the right of the door and four windows to the left. Tall windows with tightly drawn dark drapes. The old house seemed to exude a sense of withdrawal. As if the inhabitants didn't want to associate with the world that encroached on their doorstep.

"Who lives here?" Libby asked, rather surprised when, instead of knocking, Joe took a heavy key out of his pocket and unlocked the door.

"No one at the moment. A friend of my father's inherited it from his mother."

"His mother!" She allowed him to push her over the threshold, squinting into the dusky gloom. "How old is this friend of your father?"

"Dad's age." He flipped on the hall light switch, but nothing happened.

"No electricity?"

"More likely no light bulbs." He moved into the enormous living room to their right and switched on a small lamp set on the marble-topped table beside the door. It flared to life, but it's twenty-five watts didn't make an appreciable difference in the dim interior of the huge room.

"Try pulling the drapes," she suggested.

He strode across the threadbare Aubusson and yanked open the faded burgundy velvet curtains.

Libby coughed as a cloud of dust rose from the ragged material.

"How old was the lady who lived here?" she asked curiously.

"Mid-nineties, but she was bedridden for at least the last ten years."

"At which time the housekeeper quit cleaning the downstairs?" she guessed shrewdly.

"It sure looks like it, doesn't it?" Joe wiped his dusty hands on his jeans. "When Farkie used to talk about it . . ."

"Who?"

"Dad's friend, Farkie Worthington. Short for Farquahar."

"And I thought Liberty was bad," she said chortling.

"At any rate," he continued, "Farkie is going to put the place on the market and I thought you might like to see it."

Why? The question burned on the tip of her tongue, but mathematicians never jump to conclusions. She firmly squelched both the question and her bubbling excitement. Simply because he'd brought her to this house didn't mean anything. He might have thought she'd like to see an authentic mansion. And it was worth seeing, she admitted.

"May I just wander around?"

"Certainly, there's no one here to disturb. Not even a caretaker at the moment."

She meandered through the huge double living room, peeked into a book-lined study easily five times the size of her own, gave a cursory glance to the small, nondescript dining room and the two small sitting rooms behind the study and ended up in the kitchen.

"Good Lord! What a mess." She grimaced at the crumbling plaster, the water-stained ceiling and the ripped linoleum floor. Food was still scattered on the wobbly table, and the doors to the room's few cabinets hung open drunkenly. "There's less counter space than my tiny kitchen and almost no storage."

"There's a pantry through there." Joe pointed at the door to their left and Libby looked in. Ceiling-to-floor shelves held a dusty assortment of cans and bottles. She sneezed at the overpowering smell of mildew. "Where do those two doors go?" She pointed to the far wall.

"The first one goes to the basement and the other one leads to a good-sized room the housekeeper used. What do you think?" He started to lean back against the counter, took a good look at its filthy surface and thought better of the idea.

"I don't think a thing's been changed in here since the twenties." She frowned at the chipped, stained kitchen sink. "And another thing. You may not have noticed, but there isn't a john on the whole first floor!"

"That could be a problem." His eyes gleamed with laughter. "What else would you do besides install a few johns?"

"Well, for starters, I'd gut the kitchen, knock out the wall into the housekeeper's room and remodel from scratch. That way you could have a big kitchen with a comfortable dining area. Maybe with French doors. What's in back?" She pulled aside the dark green vinyl blind that covered the window over the kitchen sink, and brightened when she saw the brick-walled yard.

"Perfect." She sighed. "There's lots of room for a small patio and big flower garden."

"And a sandbox and swing set."

"For the six kids," she added. Somehow Joe's hypothetical children seemed almost alive in this old, slumbering house. "And speaking of those kids you're so keen on, you ought to knock out the wall between those two smallish sitting rooms and make one big recreation room."

"And pray it wasn't a support wall." He grinned at her.

"Can I look upstairs?"

"Sure, the back stairs are there." He pointed to a small door in the corner, which she hadn't noticed.

Libby flung open the door and frowned at the steep steps rising into the semidarkness. "Someone could break their neck on these things."

"These were originally the servants' stairs and in those days servants weren't of any great concern." He followed her up, a steadying hand on the small of her back.

They emerged into a long narrow hallway lit by a single forty-watt bulb dangling from the ceiling. The walls had been papered—from the look of it fifty years earlier—with red flowers on a cream background. The hardwood floor was dotted with a profusion of threadbare throw rugs.

"You know, this house is an anomaly." Libby began to open the doors that lined both sides of the hall.

"Why?"

"Because the outside is in perfect shape. New paint, modern storm windows, beautifully kept, but the inside . . ." She gestured toward the small cell-like room filled with moldy cardboard boxes. "Inside it looks like a once-well-to-do person who was desperately maintaining appearances at all costs."

"Looks can be deceiving. Both Farkie and his mother were millionaires many times over. The disparity is because she refused to allow him inside the house. He maintained the outside, but that was the best he could do."

"How sad. He…" Libby was diverted as she opened a door to find the house's one bathroom.

"Oh my!" She gaped in disbelief at the deep, old-fashioned tub set in a mahogany box. "This place could certainly use renovating, but whoever does it will want to be careful not to destroy its charm."

"What charm?" Joe coughed in the dust-laden air.

"It does have charm," she insisted. "It just needs freeing. Like those bedrooms. If you knocked out some walls you could have a few good-sized rooms instead of all those dark cubbyholes."

"But we need six bedrooms besides the master suite. One for each kid."

"Like I said, a couple of good-sized rooms." Libby scrubbed a spot clean on the dusty window and stared down into the garden below. What was Joe playing at? He talked as if he was planning on buying this house and remodeling it himself. Or was this merely a continuation of the game of "contract" they were playing? Or was he considering buying this house as an investment and using the event to further confuse his father, to say nothing of her? She had no way of knowing without asking and she couldn't think of a casual way to do that.

She pressed closer to the window, managing to get dirt all over her forehead as she noticed the roof below. "The second floor doesn't cover the first. That's the kitchen roof, isn't it?"

"Has to be. You know," he mused, "we could put in a huge skylight over the island work space."

"Sounds lovely," she said uncertainly, unsure of what her role was supposed to be. Not for anything would she say something to give him the idea that she felt because they'd made love he was obligated to her in some manner. She had more pride than that. Besides, she stoutly told herself, she didn't want him to be obligated. Who wanted a husband with his archaic viewpoint? She'd wind up stuck at home with a brood of kids and a terminal case of cabin fever. But what a way to go. The vivid memory of his lovemaking heated her blood and sent a flush to her cheeks. She took a deep breath trying to stem her rising tide of desire. In the process she inhaled a lungful of dust from the faded brown curtains. In her ensuing coughing fit, her awareness of Joe as a sensual being faded.

"Here." He handed her a clean handkerchief that smelled faintly of a very expensive cologne. "Wipe your face. Your tears are smearing the dirt."

Libby rubbed her cheeks, leaving a dark smudge on the pristine whiteness. She glanced down at it in dismay. "Maybe I should wash it?"

"Not here," he said, vetoing the idea. "The water's turned off. Come on, I'll run you home and you can tell me about the kids who are coming tomorrow."

"What's to tell?" She allowed him to shepherd her down the broad front staircase, hiding the sense of jubilation his words had caused. He hadn't forgotten their agreement. "They're just four little boys: two, four, five and seven. You wouldn't be trying to use that design problem as an excuse to weasel out, would you?" she asked suspiciously.

"Hardly." He looked affronted. "I agreed and I'll keep my word, if for no other reason than to prove to you that taking care of children is very rewarding." He opened the front door and motioned her outside.

"Besides," he added as he fiddled with the lock, "I brought the design home with me to work on. Once I've fed them, they should be good until lunchtime. You are bringing a few of their favorite toys along, aren't you?"

"I'll bring something." Libby forbore telling him that their favorite playthings were either illegal or antisocial. For a brief second she felt a flash of guilt at what she was about to do to Joe, but she firmly squelched it. He needed to learn a lesson, and anyway what she was doing to him was nothing compared to what he wanted to do to her. Let him find out the unpalatable reality of child care for himself. Hopefully it might shake loose some of his cast-iron views.

"HERE!" Seven-year-old Todd glanced around the luxurious lobby of Joe's apartment house, his interested gaze settling on the security guard who greeted Libby by name. "He must be as rich as some of those guys on television."

"Nah!" five-year-old Tom sneered. If he's so rich, why's he baby-sitting us?"

"I told you." Libby sat the shopping bag full of the boys' things down beside the elevator, loosened her death grip on two-year-old Timmy and turned to the three older children trailing her. "Mr. Landowski is doing this as a favor to me. And never make comments about people's money or lack thereof. It's..." She paused and peered closer at four-year-old Teddy's chubby face. "How did you get so . . . ? That's chocolate! Where did you get chocolate at seven-thirty in the morning?" She began to rummage in her purse for a Kleenex.

"The nice lady on the bus give it to me."

"What?" Libby gasped. "You know your mother told you never to take candy from a stranger."

"Oh, no." Teddy's small features assumed an expression of angelic innocence. "She said I was never to take anything from a stranger when I was alone. And I wasn't alone. You and Timmy were in the seat right in front of me," he added virtuously.

Libby, unimpressed by his logic, began to scrub the smeared chocolate off his face.

"Does he have servants?" Todd looked curiously around the luxurious lobby.

"Just a cleaning lady." Libby dashed his hopes.

"Did he sell his soul?" Tom whispered furtively.

Libby glanced up, nonplussed. "What . . . ?"

"Wibby! Go potty. Now!" Timmy wailed.

"Oh, no. Don't you have a diaper on?" She picked him up and hurried into the elevator with the three older boys right behind her.

"Hold it, Timmy," she begged. She wanted to teach Joe a lesson, but not until after she'd left for work.

"Mama says that he'll never get trained as long as he has the security of diapers," Todd rattled off what was obviously an oft-repeated sentence.

"I'm more worried about my security," Libby muttered as the elevator slid to a halt on the eleventh floor.

"Wibby!" Timmy wailed.

"Just one more minute." She raced down the hallway to 11-D and pounded the door.

After what seemed like an interminable wait, it swung open to reveal Joe. His golden hair glistened damply, a pale blue knit shirt was stretched tautly over his muscular chest and soft denim jeans hugged his powerful thighs. But for once Libby was oblivious to his overpowering masculinity.

"We need the bathroom."

"Make yourself at home," he called after her as she rushed down the hallway.

Five minutes later she was back, a now-happy Timmy beside her. She found Joe, shirtless, kneeling in a circle of small boys. A softening sensation began to grow deep in her abdomen at the sight.

"What's going on?" she asked as Teddy leaned closer to Joe's bare chest.

"We wanted to see where they took it out," Todd told her, "but it doesn't look any different."

"Took what out?"

"His soul."

"What?"

"You said he had a cleaning lady," Todd replied as if astounded by her denseness.

"Joe Landowski, would you please tell me what's going on?"

"How would I know. They're your cousins. They simply surrounded me and demanded that I take my shirt off."

"Why did you?"

"It seemed a harmless enough request." He shrugged and she watched enthralled as the muscles of his shoulders rippled beneath his supple skin. "But they're obviously disappointed."

They may have been, but she sure wasn't. She swallowed a sigh of regret as he slipped his shirt back on. Curiously, she turned to the boys.

"What does a cleaning lady have to do with anything?"

"Mom told Daddy that she'd sell her soul for a cleaning lady and since he has one, we wanted to see where the devil took it out," Tom said.

"Selling your soul to the devil is just an expression," Libby tried to explain over the roar of Joe's deep laughter. "All your mother meant was that she'd very much like a cleaning lady. You can't really sell your soul to the devil," she added at their dubious expressions.

"You can't?" Todd persisted.

"No," she repeated, and turned to the chuckling Joe. "Allow me to introduce your guests. This is Todd, Tom, Ted and Timmy." Her hand briefly rested on Timmy's white curls. "Boys, this is Mr. Landowski."

"How do you do?" they chorused, their mother's training briefly surfacing.

"Why don't you boys have a seat while I finish breakfast." Joe gestured toward the sofa.

Libby, who'd never known all four of them to be quiet at the same time, held her tongue. Let him find out things for himself.

"You got a television?" Tom demanded.

"Sure." Joe opened a walnut cabinet to reveal a twenty-five-inch screen and, more importantly from the boys' point of view, a VCR.

"Oh, boy!" Todd exclaimed, gloating. "What you got to put in it?"

"Let me see . . ." Joe opened another cabinet to reveal an impressive collection of tapes. He glanced at his diminutive guests, then back at the films. "How about one of the Muppet movies? I've got all three."

"You do?" Libby's attention was caught.

"I like the Muppets," Joe admitted sheepishly.

"Me, too. Gonzo's my favorite."

"Yuck! That's for babies." Todd's voice was scathing. "We want a real movie. One with lots of action."

"Translated, that means lots of blood and gore," Libby told Joe.

"They'll have nightmares," Joe told her.

Libby looked at him pityingly. Her young cousins didn't have nightmares, they gave them.

"How about—" she studied the titles "—this one?"

"*The Hobbit*?" Joe pulled it out and glanced uncertainly at the four small faces looking up at him.

"Go ahead. Play it," she insisted. "It'll settle them in."

"If you think so." He clearly still had his doubts, but he inserted the tape and started the machine. "What time do you have to leave?"

Libby glanced at her watch as she followed him into the kitchen. "My first class isn't for almost an hour. I thought I'd stick around for a few minutes in case they found you strange."

"Me, strange?" Joe gave her a sardonic glance that she met with one of bland innocence. "I'm beginning to think that those little protégés of yours could have convinced Spock to become a veterinarian."

"Nonsense, they're perfectly normal little boys." She quieted her conscience with the thought that they could well be perfectly normal little boys. After all, with her limited experience, what did she know?

"Breakfast is about ready." He slid the bacon into the microwave and poured the beaten eggs into a pan.

Libby sniffed appreciatively at the heavenly smell of the yeast that hung over the cooling coffee cake sitting on the table. A table set for six places. Her heart warmed at the evidence of all the trouble he'd gone to for them.

She poured herself a cup of his delicious coffee and watched him stir the creamy eggs. She rarely ate breakfast, but this smelled much too good to pass up.

He deftly transferred the eggs to a serving dish and set it on the table. "Why don't you call the boys, Libby, while I pour the orange juice."

"Sure." She found them glued to the television much as she'd expected. She pushed the stop button, told them to wash their hands and returned to the kitchen.

The boys arrived thirty seconds later, making her wonder how effective their hand washing had been, but in the interest of peace she held her tongue. No germ would have a chance against her cousins. She settled Timmy on a chair, then turned to the boys who were standing behind her. "Have a seat."

"Can we eat in front of the television?" Todd demanded.

"No." Joe's flat refusal obviously surprised them. But only for a second.

"We don't want to miss any of the movie," Tom tried.

"You won't. I stopped it." Libby explained. "It'll start up right where you left off. Now sit down."

"Not hungry," Teddy muttered, "full of chocolate."

"Then talk to us while we eat." Joe was briskly unsympathetic.

"Mommy says that children should be seen and not heard," Todd related piously.

"Yes." Joe nodded. "Having made your acquaintance I can well understand where she came by that philosophy."

"Want cereal!" Timmy shrieked. "Not that!" He glared at his plate.

"What's wrong with scrambled eggs and bacon?" Joe made the tactical error of getting into a discussion.

Libby, with the wisdom born of countless circular arguments, intervened.

"You may please yourself as to whether or not you eat it, but you will not leave the table until everyone is finished."

"Ahh, Libby!" Ted pouted.

"Sit." She pointed to a vacant chair and he slipped into it, grumbling beneath his breath. Libby ignored him. After all, she wasn't going to be the one caught in his retribution. Joe was. The thought made her grin as she sipped her coffee.

Joe shot her a suspicious look that she met blandly.

"This ain't too bad." Tom looked up at them over a half-eaten pecan caramel roll. "Not as good as my mom's, but she buys hers from the grocery store. Can't you afford to buy rolls?"

"Buy boxed rolls?" Joe looked horrified.

"Libby said we wasn't supposed to mention money!" Tod hissed at his brother.

"Oh, sorry." Tom shot a guilty look at her.

"I—" Joe broke off as the doorbell rang to the accompan-
iment of a loud thumping on his front door. "Who could that
be at this hour?" He tossed down his napkin and stood up.
"*You're* the only person I know who announces herself like
that." He strode to the front door followed by a curious Libby
and the four boys.

Joe swung open his door to reveal a furiously angry man
of about sixty. He waved his fist as Joe and Libby swallowed
their giggles. The man looked ludicrous. Like a bantam
rooster taking on a tiger.

"Stop it! Right now!" he screamed.

"Stop what?" Joe asked, keeping his temper under control
with an almost visible effort.

"The water!" The bright red hue of the man's face was beginning to alarm Libby. She wanted to annoy Joe, not drive
one of his neighbors into a heart attack.

"Exactly what's the problem?" she asked soothingly.

"I live in the apartment beneath you and the water in your
bathroom is overflowing."

"What?" Joe looked incredulous.

"Oh-oh," Libby heard Ted mutter, and an awful premonition came to her. She raced for the bathroom a step ahead of
Joe. She knew her suspicions had been correct the minute her
shoes sank with a strangled gurgle into the wet plush carpet.

"Oh no!" Libby dived for the toilet that was sending a
steady stream of clear water pouring onto the floor. She in-
effectively jiggled the lever, but Joe pushed past her, lifted the
tank lid and pulled something inside. The flow stopped immediately.

"I'll send you the bill for repairing my ceiling and replacing the wet wallpaper." The man stared at Joe as if expecting
an argument. When he didn't get one, he contented himself
with one final glare and left.

"How did this happen?" Libby demanded of the boys who
were tentatively poking their toes into the soaking carpet.

"Timmy put a whole roll of paper in the toilet," Ted related.

"And you flushed it?" she asked incredulously.

"Of course I didn't," Ted denied. "Timmy did."

"Me," Timmy gleefully confessed. "Went woosh." He smiled happily at the memory.

"Never mind how it happened." Joe looked helplessly around the drenched bathroom. "The question is what do we do now?"

Libby glanced at her watch. "Call a plumber I guess. I'd love to stay and help, but I have to be in my office in thirty minutes."

"What?" Joe shouted.

"You were the one who said raising kids provided lots of scope," she pointed out. "So you solve the problem."

"These aren't kids!" Joe glared at the four boys. "They're imps of Satan."

"Wanna watch movie," Timmy yelled.

"Go, with my blessings." Joe sighed heavily.

"And I'm going to work." She smiled at him as she left, ignoring his mutter of 'quisling.' This would be a good experience for him, she told herself firmly. She was really doing him a favor by showing him what large closely spaced families could be like.

10

LIBBY SHIFTED HER BRIEFCASE from her right to her left hand and pushed the button for the eleventh floor. She leaned back against the elevator's oak paneling and idly wondered what she would find when she reached Joe's apartment. She'd spent the day alternating between feelings of guilt at what she'd let him in for and a gleeful anticipation of the shattering of his ridiculous assumption that spending the day surrounded by four young children was mentally stimulating. The boys were stimulating all right. They were more than capable of stimulating him right out of his mind.

The elevator halted obediently on the eleventh floor and Libby got off. She paused in front of his door, cautiously listening, but she could hear nothing within. Was it possible the boys were taking a nap? The fantastic idea occurred to her only to be instantly dismissed. In the first place it was four o'clock, much too late for an afternoon nap. And in the second, her cousin assured her that the boys had given up naps long ago, even Timmy.

Taking a deep breath, Libby gently depressed the doorbell. Joe's remark about her normal method of announcing her arrival still rankled. To her surprise, the door swung open immediately.

Joe stared at her like a drowning man suddenly thrown a lifeline. He grabbed her arm and yanked her inside as if he was afraid that she might change her mind and leave.

"Where the hell have you been?"

"It's only four o'clock," she replied mildly. "Most men don't get home until after six."

"If their kids are anything like those four—" he cast a scorching glance toward the living room "—then I'm surprised they come home at all."

"Where are the boys?" she asked cautiously.

"Watching *The Hobbit*. They've been watching it all day long." His eyes momentarily glazed. "Over and over. I know the damn thing by heart!"

"How about a cup of coffee?" She thought it prudent to change the subject.

"Come out into the kitchen. The sound of the movie's muted out there."

Libby peered into the living room as he hustled her toward the kitchen. The boys were huddled two feet from the front of the television, watching with enthralled interest.

"Is it wise to let them sit that close?" she asked, trying to remember an article she'd read about the subject. "Mightn't it cause problems with their eyes later on?"

"Don't worry. They'll never live to grow up," he said emphatically.

Libby swallowed a grin. From the sound of his voice, things must have gone pretty much as she'd expected them to.

"Evening, boys," she called to them.

"Shh," Tom admonished. "This is the good part."

"Yeah, they're going to have this big battle and the old guy is going to get covered with blood," Todd elaborated with ghoulish relish.

"Oh?" She blinked uncertainly as Joe pulled her through the kitchen door.

"Where . . . ?" Libby turned to him, gasping in surprise as his strong arms closed around her slight body, yanking her up against him. The breath rushed out of her lungs as the feel of his hard muscles intruded into her soft flesh. She tilted her head back to ask him what he was doing and found her mouth captured by his mobile lips. There was nothing tentative or gentle about the kiss. It seemed to be motivated by a deep driving need that demanded immediate satisfaction. His tongue thrust inside, aggressively exploring the velvety moistness behind her teeth while his arms tightened, as if trying to absorb her into him.

Joyously she welcomed the invasion, allowing him to bind her to him. A languorous desire sparked to life deep within her, and she pressed her hips against his muscled thighs. A faint tremor chased over her skin at the hardening warmth of him. The raspy feel of his day's growth of beard brushed tantalizingly over her soft chin and the fiery taste of brandy on his breath flavored the kiss. Long before she'd sated her throbbing senses on the taste and feel of him, he raised his head and looked down into her blue eyes, still cloudy with the strength of the desire churning through her. He dropped a final kiss on her nose and gently released her.

"I needed that!" He sighed in satisfaction.

Libby expelled her breath and tried to will away the disoriented feeling his kiss had engendered. She allowed the scalding cup of coffee he handed her to remain on the counter, afraid that her trembling fingers would betray her if she tried to pick it up. She watched as he filled a glass from a half-empty bottle of cognac and took a hefty swallow. She frowned thoughtfully.

"It's kind of early for that, isn't it?"

"It was too late the minute you wished those demons on me."

"I take it that the day has not met with your preconceived notions?"

"It met them and promptly destroyed them." He groaned. "Once the plumber had finished and the cleaners had removed the dripping carpet, it was almost lunchtime. Since they'd already seen *The Hobbit* two and a half times, I naively assumed that they'd like to do something else."

"Such as?" she asked cautiously.

"Eat lunch at McDonald's and spend the afternoon at the zoo."

"You took them out of the apartment?" she asked apprehensively.

"Your concern is well placed. It's a shame that you didn't bother telling me this morning that they aren't civilized."

"They are, too." She defended them halfheartedly. "They're just rather . . . rather high spirited."

"They're brats!" he corrected her emphatically. "Tom tried to feed the elephant the toy car he had in his pocket."

"Oh, dear." Libby winced.

"Yes. 'Oh, dear,'" Joe repeated sardonically. "And he did it right in front of the attendant. We were none too politely requested to remove ourselves from the premises."

"Sorry about that," she sincerely apologized. She'd wanted to teach him a lesson about kids, not publicly humiliate him.

"Me, too. At that point I gave up. I brought them back here, put *The Hobbit* back in the VCR and hid out in the kitchen."

"You didn't find any scope for your talents?" She was unable to resist the gibe.

"I'm not dumb!" He glared at her. "An idiot could see that this was set up to convince me that kids are bad news."

"Not precisely. Just a lot of them close together."

"But you're forgetting something, Libby. If they were ours, they'd never have been allowed to develop the way they have. All those kids want to do is to watch television. Even the baby!" He was outraged. "They can tell you what's on any channel in the city at any given time. Your cousin is a menace."

"No." Libby shook her head. "She's simply a tired, put-upon wife and mother. She wasn't always like that. When there was simply Todd, she was always taking him on outings to the zoo, the museums, the park. Even when Tom came along two years later she still managed to do lots of things with them. When Ted was born a year later, it all got to be too much for her, but she still tried. It wasn't until Timmy was born two years ago that she simply gave up. They live in a small apartment in Manhattan and to keep them quiet she fell into the trap of using television as a tranquilizer."

"Hmm." He frowned thoughtfully at the information.

"But the point is that she wasn't always like that. It was too many babies too fast that changed her. The boys might infuriate me on occasions, but basically I feel very sorry for them as well as for their mother. They're all caught in a vicious cycle."

"At least one thing was accomplished today." He frowned thoughtfully into his glass. "I now know that there's a definite reason behind your refusal to have a large family. Even if your concern is misguided. No, think a minute," he continued when she started to refute what he was saying, "by basing your views on large families on your cousin's experience, you're comparing apples and oranges. You wouldn't have the total responsibility for our kids the way your cousin does. You'd have a housekeeper and a full-time nanny."

"With the end result that my kids would get their values from the hired help," Libby shot back. "If we had one child, I would have lots of time to spend with him in the evenings and on weekends. Maybe even with two, although I have my doubts. But more than that and the nanny is raising my kids, and don't tell me to quit my job because I won't do it," she added firmly. "I prefer the proven satisfaction of teaching to the dubious joys of full-time motherhood."

"Your job means that much to you?"

"At last you're getting the idea!"

"How about teaching part-time?"

"It wouldn't work." She shook her head. "Part-time professors are low men on the totem pole. They get the assignments no one else wants. It's taken me years to work up to the classes I now have. If I went on part-time, I'm liable to wind up teaching freshman algebra." She shuddered, remembering earlier horrors.

"Perhaps..." he began thoughtfully, then Tom burst into the room.

"Joe! Joe! We can't get the tape to rewind."

"It doesn't matter," Libby said. "I promised your mother I'd have you home by five, so we have to be leaving."

"Ah, Libby! We want to see it again."

"No." She shook her head. "Go turn off the television and tell your brothers we're leaving."

"But, Libby..." he wailed.

"You heard your cousin." Joe's emphatic tone brooked no argument and Tom retreated.

"Come on. Let's return that quartet to their mother."

"You don't have to come with us." She forced herself to make the offer, despite the fact that she very much wanted to have him along.

"I wouldn't send a convicted terrorist out alone with them, let alone you."

Libby cautiously searched the rugged planes of his face, not really certain what she was looking for. What had he meant, let alone her? Her gaze became entangled in the tiny lights gleaming deep in his bright blue eyes. Just maybe the cataclysmic experience they'd shared meant something more to him than momentary gratification. Maybe it meant as much as it did to her, she thought, admitting the truth that lay deep within her.

Todd rushed into the kitchen. "Can we take *The Hobbit* home with us?".

"You haven't got a VCR to play it on," Libby said.

"Sometimes we rent one," Todd replied hopefully.

"Let him take it." Joe sighed. "I'll never be able to watch it again without shuddering."

"Thanks!" Todd beamed at him. "I guess you aren't so bad after all." He ran back toward the living room.

"No." She smiled at him. "You aren't."

"Actually, I'm trying to get on your good side. I want a favor. A business associate of mine from the Midwest called this afternoon. He's flying in on Saturday to attend a fabric show that starts next week."

"Yes?" Libby prompted with a sense of foreboding. Surely Joe wasn't going to pass her along to someone else, was he? A chill iced her skin as she waited for his next words.

"He'll be at loose ends Saturday night, and I thought you might ask that cute brunette to come along and we'll entertain him."

"Cute brunette?" she asked cautiously, not certain who was to be whose date. For all she knew, he'd been taken with Jessie and was using this outing as an attempt to get to know her better.

His answer reassured her. "I can't remember her name, but she was in your apartment the day I took you to the beach. We could take them to a Broadway show and then to the Alhambra for dancing."

"Sounds like fun." Relief lent brilliance to her voice. Jessie was for his associate. Joe had automatically aligned himself with her. "I'd love to go. I'll check with Jessie once you drop me and the boys off."

"Check after we have supper." He encircled her shoulders with a large arm and briefly pulled her into his side. He dropped a kiss on her tousled curls. "Hmm, your hair smells like sunshine."

"Not surprising," she forced a prosaic answer, although she was unable to stop her body clinging to his warm flesh. "That sun outside is strong enough to blister paint."

"Or burn skin." A frown colored his voice.

Libby shivered as his warm lips began to nuzzle the back of her neck. She was certain she could feel her bones slowly dissolving as his mouth wandered slowly over the sensitive area behind her ear. "Joe, I . . ." A blissful sigh shook her as his strong white teeth began to nibble her earlobe.

"I thought you said we gotta go!" Todd's voice accused.

"Yes," Joe murmured softly against her tender flesh, "you most definitely have to go."

"Shh." Libby hastily pulled out of his arms, for some reason shy at being watched. "You'll hurt his feelings," she chided Joe, ignoring his incredulous expression.

A wonderful feeling of euphoria filled her. He wanted to buy her supper after the day's fiasco. He definitely was fond of her.

"WHAT'S JOE'S FRIEND'S NAME?" Jessie fiddled with one of her pearl earrings.

"I can't remember if he told me." Full of last-minute doubts about her choice of dress, Libby frowned at her reflection in the living room mirror. Her glance swept over the floor-length skirt of black silk, coming to rest on the matching camisole top. Miniscule straps held up the deeply cut bodice, while strategically placed black lace inserts provided tantalizing glimpses of her pale curved breasts. It was a sophisticated gown that required a certain amount of panache to carry it off, and suddenly she not only felt very unsophisticated but strangely uncertain in the bargain. Maybe she should have opted for something a little more conventional.

"What are you grimacing about?" Jessie demanded. "I'm the one with cause for concern. Lord, I haven't been on a blind date since I was in high school. I'm giving you fair warning; if this guy turns out to be a turkey, I'm going to spend the evening making eyes at Joe. Not that I'd have a chance." She sighed in good-natured envy. "You look spectacular."

"You think so?" Libby tried draping the cobwebby black silk evening shawl over her bare shoulders.

"Are you kidding! That dress would cause heart palpitations in a ninety-year-old man, let alone that gorgeous hunk you're dating."

"It isn't too . . . ?" Libby gestured toward her barely covered breasts.

"Yes, it is." Jessie nodded emphatically. "That's what makes it so special."

"I don't know." She nervously patted the elaborate Grecian knot that confined her gleaming hair.

"What's with you? You've worn that dress before."

"I know but . . ."

"You couldn't be falling for this Landowski, could you?" Jessie looked horrified.

"Of course not!" she emphatically denied, even as a line from *Hamlet*, "The lady doth protest too much, methinks," echoed in her ears. Fortunately the doorbell rang, diverting Jessie from a line of thought that Libby didn't want explored.

"Wait a second!" Jessie hurriedly sank down into a seductive pose on the sofa, arranging her cardinal-red skirt in graceful folds. "Do I look languid?" She leaned provocatively back against the sofa, the soft swell of her breasts clearly outlined beneath the tightly fitting red silk bodice.

"To the point of consumption." Libby grinned at her friend and opened the door to the sound of Jessie's smothered laughter.

Libby's eyes widened in startled appreciation as she feasted on the sight of Joe. A Joe she barely recognized. His broad shoulders were covered by a superbly cut evening jacket. Its midnight hue seemed to emphasize the gleaming brightness of his blond hair. Approvingly she noted his pristine white shirt; it's very starkness gave him a dignity that no amount of fashionable ruffles could attain. Evening clothes suited Joe, but they also gave him an unfamiliar dimension, she realized uneasily, making him appear slightly out of focus. As if he was a stranger she'd suddenly stumbled across. Uncertainly, her eyes traveled up past his broad chest, over his square, clean-shaven chin and lingered longingly on his firm lips before sweeping upward to become entangled in the blaze of desire burning brightly in the depths of his blue eyes. An answering glow sparked to life within her, but before she could say anything, the man standing to the left and slightly behind Joe, whom she hadn't even noticed, spoke up.

"Well, hel . . . lo there, honey." The man's slightly protuberant brown eyes seemed riveted to her curves. "If you aren't a sight for sore eyes." His pudgy hand reached out to pat her arm and Libby instinctively recoiled. "And who might you be?" He didn't seem to have noticed her reaction.

"This is Libby Michalowski." Joe stepped inside. His arm encircled her shoulders, possessively pulling her up against his side. The faint roughness of his jacket raised prickles of awareness on her bare skin and she pressed against him, relishing the erotic friction.

"And where do you find someone as cute as her?" The man's eyes remained glued to her décolletage.

"My father introduced us," Joe said severely, and Libby swallowed a giggle at the man's crestfallen expression.

"Oh." He seemed momentarily nonplussed. "Sorry, I misunderstood. I should have known that a cute little thing like you would be taken."

"Libby, this is Ed Walton."

"Ed." She tentatively shook his hand.

"Yup, Ed's my name and fabric's my game."

"How . . . ?" She groped for a suitable reply, found none and instead motioned him into the living room.

"Ed, I'd like to introduce Jessie Anders. Jessie, Ed Walton."

"I should have known." Ed sighed rapturously. "Such a cute thing as Libby here would only surround herself with beauty to match her own. Dare I hope that you are to be my date for the night?" He clutched the front of his slightly rumpled maroon evening jacket and his eyes bulged hopefully at Jessie.

Libby caught Jessie's incredulous expression and hastily looked away before she broke into laughter.

"Ice," she muttered. "I need ice for the drinks." She escaped into the kitchen, shamelessly abandoning the stunned Jessie. She hurriedly flipped on the water in the kitchen sink to muffle the sounds of her strangled giggles. She turned to find that Joe had followed her.

"Ed's not that bad, although I will admit that I didn't care for the way he was eyeing you at first." His face unexpectedly tightened with annoyance.

"As long as it's just his eyes he's free with." Libby shrugged and the silken material slithered over her skin.

"Any normal male is going to respond to you in that outfit," Joe murmured softly as his large hand cupped her shoulder. His thumb pressed into the base of her neck and slowly, insidiously, he began to massage the tiny pulse point hammering with frantic life.

"And he is right." His voice deepened ever so slightly. "I've never seen anything so exquisite as your creamy skin in stark relief against that clinging black silk." He paused as his hand slipped lower, hovering over her breast. Her breathing developed an uneven cadence as he deliberately cupped the straining flesh, slowly kneading it through the sleek material. Her breath whistled past her softly parted lips and she swayed toward him. Her eyes slid shut, the better to concentrate on the feel of his moving fingers. Her burgeoning desire fanned a faint heat that painted her pale cheeks. She could feel her nipple hardening.

"You're all silk," Joe murmured against her fragrant hair. "A gorgeous silken fabric, covering an exquisite skin of satin and velvet. So soft and warm and welcoming." His hypnotic voice was seducing her mind even as his caressing hand was seducing her body. "You're everything . . ."

"Libby!" Jessie's hoarse whisper reached her a second before the kitchen door swung open.

Joe removed his hand from her breast with such speed that Libby couldn't help wondering which of them he was protecting. He wasn't a shy man and being caught making mild love to his date shouldn't have bothered him. So why had he backed off as if burned? An unanswerable question, she admitted, purposefully banishing it. Needing a second to regain her equilibrium, she opened the freezer and pulled out an ice tray.

"What's wrong, Jessie?" Libby twisted the tray into the ice bucket on the counter.

"I'll tell you what's wrong. Your friend—" she glared at Joe. "—just propositioned me."

"He what!" Libby stared at the sputtering Jessie. "How on earth did he manage to work that into the conversation in such a short time?"

"He didn't even try," Jessie said wryly. "He merely asked me to go to bed with him."

"Hell! I'm sorry, Jessie. Ed is what's known as a diamond in the rough, but I can't say that I've ever noticed him being this much in the rough before. Would you like me to take him back to his hotel?"

"And cheat me out of seeing a Broadway hit, followed by a visit to the Alhambra? Not on your life," Jessie said emphatically. "Besides, now that I think about it, his attitude's rather refreshing. It's so direct."

"So's a slug from a forty-five," Libby said dryly, picking up the full ice bucket.

"If you're certain that's what you want, we'll go, but I won't have him talking to you like that," he said. "You aren't that kind of girl. Give me five minutes alone with him before you come out, and I guarantee you won't have any more trouble with him."

"No blood!" Libby told him, "and, anyway, I kind of agree with Jessie. He's so open about his lechery that it's hard to take offense."

"I'm not having any trouble at all," Joe said sourly. "One expects a grown man to have some finesse. Remember, five minutes."

"Honestly, Libby," Jessie exclaimed as the door swung shut behind him, "life around you is never dull. What's the matter?" She frowned at the arrested expression on Libby's face.

"What he said."

"What who said?"

"Joe," Libby answered impatiently. "About you not being that kind of girl."

"That depends." Jessie twirled the end of an imaginary mustache. "With Ed, no sane woman is that kind of girl, but now with your intended . . ." Her voice trailed away suggestively.

A stab of desire so intense it was almost painful shook Libby at her words. A feeling she was quick to deny. Joe wasn't and never would be her intended. Nor did she want him to be, she told herself stoutly. He'd drive her crazy within a week.

"Did what he say really bother you that much?" Jessie asked uncertainly.

"It wasn't the comment per se. It's his habit of dropping caustic remarks like that every once in a while. And it doesn't bother me, it infuriates me. As if the world were divided into two kinds of women. Those you dally with and those you marry."

"So he's a male chauvinist pig with a shocking double standard." Jessie shrugged. "The solution is simple. Close your ears and simply look at the body. Heaven knows, he's well worth looking at. What do you care what's going on in his head?"

Because I like him and I value his friendship and because I was stupid enough to go to bed with him and as a result I may have blown everything, Libby thought desolately.

"Come on," Jessie said. "Joe's had long enough. Let's go see if there are any survivors."

Rather to Libby's surprise, she found the two men happily discussing the state of the textile industry. Whatever Joe had told Ed, it certainly hadn't angered him, but it most definitely had altered his behavior toward Jessie. He became positively avuncular and as the evening wore on his behavior bordered on the ridiculous. He spent most of the play apologizing for the rather mild swearing peppering the dialogue. During the third act he all but covered Jessie's eyes during a particularly moving love scene.

Jessie gave Libby an incredulous look, and they both turned to stare at Joe who was shaking with suppressed laughter. Frustrated, Libby glared at him, dying to know what he had said to Ed, but she could hardly start demanding answers in the middle of the play.

It wasn't until almost four hours later, after they'd dropped Ed off at his hotel and safely seen Jessie into her apartment, that Libby was able to question him. She managed to contain her impatience until they'd reached her door.

"Well?" she demanded.

"Aren't you going to ask me in?" Joe managed to look boyishly hopeful. "I'd love a nightcap."

"After this evening I need one." She unlocked her door and switched on a light. She tossed her tiny silver evening bag on the hall table, kicked off her shoes and let her shawl drop onto the carpet. Going to the liquor cabinet, she poured a measure of brandy into a small crystal glass.

Joe held out his hand for it, but Libby shook her head, standing just out of reach.

"First tell me what you threatened Ed with."

"Threatened?" He looked hurt at her charge. "I wouldn't hurt a hair on his balding head." He unfastened his tie and dropped it on the coffee table. His jacket followed and he sank down on the couch. He slipped off his shoes and propped up his large feet on her coffee table.

"Give me my drink, wench."

"Tempting." She eyed him. "Very tempting."

"I am, aren't I?" he said smugly.

"I was referring to giving you your drink. Or more specifically, to pouring it over your head. Only one thing is stopping me."

"Your basic respect for me as a person?"

"No, the fact that the liquor stains would be impossible to get out of a cream-colored fabric. Now tell me what you said to the apprentice rake."

"Merely that Jessie had decided to renounce the world and she'd been accepted as a novice by the Sisters of St. Joseph and would be reporting to the mother house next month." He looked pleased with himself.

"Joseph Landowski!" Libby gaped at him. "You're lucky you weren't struck with a bolt of lightning on the spot."

"Wrong theology." He took the cognac from her limp hand and then tugged her down beside him.

"But the nuns . . ."

"Well, you wouldn't let me hit him," he reminded her. "And I didn't have much time. Besides, this way didn't hurt his feelings."

"I suppose." She offered no resistance as he pulled her up against him.

"It worked."

"Rather too well. Poor Jessie didn't even get to dance if you remember correctly."

"Women!" he groaned. "First, you complain because he's overly familiar and then you complain because he isn't familiar enough."

"All we wanted was a happy medium."

"Happy medium?" He took a swallow of his drink and then set it down on the end table.

"Let's explore that concept in a little more depth." His left arm suddenly yanked her up against his chest and his mouth swooped down, closing over hers with implacable intent. Deliberately he pressed her hips against his body, his tongue aggressively thrusting into her mouth.

Libby shuddered under the onslaught as a thousand separate sensations bombarded her mind. It was impossible to fully respond to them and she moaned in frustration. It was like being forced to gulp down a rare vintage wine instead of being allowed to savor each delicate sip.

His arms suddenly slackened and Libby blinked up into his bright blue eyes, trying to clear her passion-fogged senses.

"What do you think?"

"Think?" she parroted, formulating thoughts being an impossible task at the moment.

"Was that a happy medium?"

"No." She took a deep breath and filled her lungs with air, trying to respond to this teasing. "Too far on the side of domination."

"Mmm." His eyes gleamed with a bedeviling light that she instinctively mistrusted. "Let's move down the scale a little."

"This is no laughing matter, Joe Landowski."

"That's the understatement of the year," he murmured obscurely as he drew her back into his arms. Only this time he gently folded her up against him as if relishing the action. Their bodies were barely touching as he began to drop tiny, tormenting kisses over her jawline, working his way around to her right ear, where he nuzzled the soft sensitive area behind the lobe.

"Joe..." Her voice quavered as her skin flamed beneath his questing lips, and strong white teeth began to nibble on her ear lobes. Blindly Libby sought his mouth, but his large hands captured her head, holding it still.

"Patience."

She could hear the husky note in his voice as she fumbled with his shirt buttons with fingers feeling strangely clumsy At last they yielded to her inept handling and with a sigh of pleasure, she slipped her hand inside, gasping as the hair on his chest grazed her palm. Her skin absorbed the sensation, amplifying it. She flexed her fingers in the crisp pelt, tugging ever so slightly.

His gasp of pleasure encouraged her and Libby allowed her hand to wander. Her fingers probed the hard muscles of his chest, coming to rest on the flat nipples almost buried in the thick blond fur. She flicked the top of one with her nail and smiled dreamily at the shudder that shook his large frame.

"You're an enchantress. The exquisite distillation of whatever it is that makes a woman feminine." His tender voice stroked the passion escalating in her loins while his hand explored the satiny skin of her neck and then traced the fragile line of her collarbone.

A sob of pleasure shook her as he gently pushed the thin strap over her shoulder.

"I've been aching to do that all evening," he breathed as his unsteady fingers slowly pulled the silk bodice down, baring her small breast. His hand cupped the warm flesh, and his thumb gently bushed over the dusky-pink bud flowering under the force of her passion.

"All through that interminable play the only thing I could think of was the way your breasts moved under that shimmering silk. I knew you didn't have a thing on underneath it. It was all I could do not to drag you off into the nearest dark corner and strip it off you."

Libby shivered at the raw passion in his voice, savagely glad that he found her body as exciting as she found his.

"If possible, you feel even better than I'd imagined." He effortlessly lifted her upward and his tongue lightly licked over the soft curves of her breast.

"Joe!" Her fingers curled in his chest hair and she tried to tug him closer. His insubstantial caresses were slowly driving her out of her mind. She wanted to feel his hot mouth, to feel his hard body pressing into hers. But he didn't seem to share her sense of urgency. With tortuous slowness, the tip of his tongue painted circles around her breast as it drew ever nearer to the tip.

Her abdomen fluttered and a heavy warmth settled deep within it. Libby took a deep shuddering breath, and the fresh scent of his clean hair floated into her nostrils. She licked her dry lips and the fingertips of her free hand trailed over the hair-roughened skin of his strong jaw.

"Please..." Her whimpered plea escaped through clenched teeth and she began to shiver uncontrollably.

"What do you want, my precious Libby?" His crooning voice warmed the tip of her breast.

"For you to stop it!" she gasped.

"Stop kissing you?"

"No!" Libby moaned softly as her shivering intensified. "Stop playing games and make love to me." And mean it. The wish filtered through her jumbled thoughts. As I do. The devastating burst of self-knowledge shattered the last of her reserve and she arched into him. "Now. I need you now."

"Oh, yes, my darling girl." Joe stood, still holding her tightly against him. "I could make love to you while the world spun off its axis."

Please God, let him. The about urgent prayer filled her mind as he strode toward the bedroom and the promise of ecstasy.

11

"BEHOLD, I BRING YOU tidings of great joy." Frederic dropped the manila envelope on the restaurant's small table and sat down, beaming at his fellow conspirators.

"But not originality." Casimir leaned back in his chair.

"What's that?" Sigismund looked at the envelope.

"A cause for celebration." Frederic gestured toward the waiter and, when he came, ordered a bottle of the best champagne.

Casimir opened the envelope and slowly perused its contents while the waiter uncorked the wine.

Frederic waved the waiter away and poured the pale, sparkling liquid himself.

"Well?" Sigismund demanded of Casimir.

"It's a deed." Casimir frowned. "To a house over on—" he glanced at the top of the page "—Thirty-eighth Street."

"So, Frederic?" Sigismund asked. "You're investing in rental property?"

"Not in that neighborhood, he isn't," Casimir said thoughtfully.

"And it's not my deed," Frederic said. "It belongs to Joe. And it isn't just a house. It's a very large family house. With two full floors, a dormered attic and a big yard in the back."

"Joe bought it?" Sigismund's eyes brightened.

"Yes. He signed the papers two days ago. Not only that, but he's got an architect all lined up to begin on the remodeling. But first—" Frederic paused for effect "—he says he wants to go over his ideas with Libby."

"Very promising." Sigismund rubbed his thin hands together.

"Almost too promising." Casimir frowned.

"What is that supposed to mean?" Frederic demanded in exasperation.

"I don't know exactly. This house..." Casimir tapped the deed with his finger. "It doesn't make any sense. We know full well they're only negotiating that contract to keep you two occupied, but no one puts out the kind of money your son just did for a joke."

"I think they've gotten trapped in their own game," Frederic crowed.

"You could be right." Sigismund took a sheath of papers out of his suit jacket and passed a copy to each man. "This is the latest edition of the contract, and there's no more nonsense in it about feather mattresses."

"Hmm." Frederic glanced over the two-page document. "And they've agreed on a Catholic grade school for the kids even if the rest is still up in the air. I can almost see my grandchildren now." Frederic sighed dreamily.

"I don't like it," Casimir broke in.

"Why?" Sigismund said. "I think Frederic's right. I think they really like each other."

"I'll concede that." Casimir waved his hand dismissingly. "But I still don't like it. It's too..." He searched for words and settled for, "...easy. I simply don't believe that two such strong-willed adults can be having such an uneventful courtship. You two mark my words, it isn't going to be that easy."

"Bah!" Frederic snorted. "You're an old woman."

"Better that than an old fool," Casimir shot back.

"We shall see," Sigismund said calmly. "And we should be seeing that before too much longer. They may not realize it, but at the rate they're negotiating, the contract should only take a few more passes to complete."

"And then the wedding." Frederic declared, ignoring Casimir's disbelieving snort.

"I'D LOVE TO, JOE. I don't have anything else planned for this afternoon." Libby strove to keep her voice level. "I've already been to church and I had an early lunch. Yes, that's fine. I'll see you in about twenty minutes. Bye." She gently hung up the phone and gave way to the excitement bubbling through her. Joe had actually bought that gorgeous old house! And not only that, but he wanted her to go over it with him this afternoon to help draw up a list of specifications for the architect handling the remodeling.

But why had he bought it? That was the sixty-four-thousand dollar question. It was the timing of his purchase that bothered her most, she admitted to herself. Why buy a house at this particular point in the negotiations? But the more she thought about it, the more she had to concede that the timing had to be coincidence. Farkie's mother would hardly have died just so Joe could buy her house. Libby grimaced at the ridiculous thought. No, coincidence was the only answer. The owner had died and her heir hadn't wanted to be bothered with the redecorating necessary to bring it up to its full worth, so he'd let it go for substantially below its market value.

No doubt Joe had bought it as an investment, thinking to resell it for a substantial profit once the work was completed. A lot of people made a good living doing just that. Maybe he simply wanted her advice because she was a woman, and any woman would do. Or perhaps it was more complicated than that. Perhaps he was planning on asking her to share it with him....

No! Libby emphatically shook her head. Joe wouldn't ask the daughter of a friend of his father's to live with him. He had too much sense of what was owed his family to do that. If Joe was indeed planning on asking her to share his house, it would be within the bonds of matrimony.

A wild flare of excitement sparked to life only to flicker and die under the harsh reality of facts. She might have been stupid enough to have committed the folly of falling in love with him, but there had been no sign that her monumental act of dementia was contagious. Oh, she knew he liked her. Liked her a lot. Both as a friend and as a lover. Her heart swelled as she remembered a week ago after their ill-fated double dates, when he'd made love to her over and over again until finally toward dawn they'd both fallen asleep from exhaustion. Sexually, they were unbelievably compatible. Each seeming to know exactly what the other wanted and needed. To Libby, their lovemaking was a miracle. But tempting though the prospect was, they couldn't spend all their time in bed.

And though she might love Joe with all her heart, it didn't mean she wasn't regularly overwhelmed with an impulse to murder him. Restlessly she flung aside her drapes and stared down into the street, but there was very little activity to distract her disquieting thoughts at one o'clock on a summer Sunday afternoon.

Their ways of looking at life were so different. No matter how much pleasure she found in his company, discord always seemed to lurk right below the surface. She grimaced as she remembered Thursday. The evening had started out so pleasantly. Joe had unexpectedly been waiting for her outside her last class at the university. He'd told her that he'd finally solved his design problem and was going to the beach house for a swim to celebrate, and asked if she wanted to come along.

Delightedly she'd agreed. She'd been so happy that he'd thought of her when he'd wanted to celebrate, but her elation hadn't survived the evening. Things had started out well enough. They'd spent a pleasant two hours swimming and relaxing on the beach. It wasn't until Joe had calmly told her that he was tired after his long hard day at the office, so she could cook their dinner, that the evening had taken a turn for the worse. She had also had a long, hard day and to be expected to fix the meal simply because she was a woman had been the last straw. She'd called him a male chauvinist pig and flatly refused to do it.

Which had not been the way to approach the problem, she'd realized the minute the words left her mouth. What she should have done was to tell him simply that she was tired, too, and would appreciate some help. But her pride hadn't allowed her to plead her case. With the result that neither of them had gotten their supper. Libby giggled at the memory. They'd behaved like two spoiled brats, but at least *she* admitted it. Joe had insisted that his silence was dignified.

She took a restless turn about her living room. Her deep, abiding love for him hadn't suddenly transformed her into his ideal. Nor had it made her willing to capitulate. If anything, her knowledge of her own vulnerability had made her all the more determined not to give in to his demands.

But Joe did seem willing to compromise. Libby reminded herself of several areas of the contract where they'd managed to reach an agreement. And he'd actually seemed to understand the point she'd been trying to make by exposing him to the boys. Or perhaps he'd simply decided that it wasn't worth continuing to fight over what was in effect a game. Even though at times he seemed to forget the underlying reason for their negotiations, that didn't mean he'd fallen in love with her. And even if by some miracle he had, what could she do about it? Not much, she admitted. She could either ask him exactly how he felt about her, or she could let the situation ride and hope he'd tell her in his own good time.

For a moment she actually considered asking, only to decide against it. It was too soon to force an answer. If his initial liking for her was deepening into love, making him examine his emotions before the process was complete could be disastrous. He might decide to cut his losses while he still could.

Then, too, if his feelings really were only liking, and he was simply playing the game as they'd originally agreed, letting him know that she loved him and wanted much more from him than friendship might make him feel that he had no option but to discontinue their relationship for her sake.

And underlying everything was her unshakable conviction that confronting Joe would be a mistake. Everything she'd learned about him pointed to the fact that he was a man who did his own pursuing. As far as he was concerned, taking the initiative was solely the male prerogative.

Face it, she told herself, *you don't really know what to do. So do nothing. Simply let the present situation stand.* At least this way she got to enjoy his company several times a week.

She glanced at the clock: one-ten. Joe was due in ten minutes and, if she was planning on spending the afternoon going through his newly acquired and very dusty house, she'd be wise to change out of her Sunday best. Preferably into something old and definitely into something washable, such as jeans and a T-shirt.

She was glad she had changed—despite Joe's resigned sigh upon seeing her—when he'd unlocked the front door to the town house and swung it open. It was in even worse condition than she'd remembered, although Joe didn't seem to notice the thick coating of dust that covered everything. He merely glanced around the hall, a complacent expression of proud ownership on his face.

Libby followed him in, her steps echoing eerily as she crossed the black-and-white checkered marble floor. Cautiously, she peeked into the front living room. Sunlight poured in through the uncurtained windows, highlighting the deplorable state of the faded, peeling wallpaper and the deep gouges in the darkly stained oak flooring. Without the clutter of furniture the room seemed even bigger than it had originally. She walked over to a fireplace she had overlooked in the clutter the last time she was here.

"Very nice." She ran a fingertip along the elaborate carvings on the mantel.

"Um-hum." Joe opened the black notebook he was carrying and shifted through some papers. "According to the architect's report, it may be an authentic Adams. Do you want to keep it or replace it with something a little more modern?"

"Modern?" Libby glanced protectively at the beautiful thing. "Don't you dare change that. It's not only beautiful in its own right, but it exactly fits the room. If you'd wanted modern, you should have bought out on Oyster Bay."

"I wanted to," he reminded her. "If you'll recall you were the one so stuck on the city. Not that I don't think you were right, all things considered. And, besides, this place is starting to grow on me."

"I think what you feel is creeping mold." She sneezed as dust tickled her nose. "What about turning off the air-conditioning and opening a few windows to freshen things up a little?"

"And trade dust for car exhaust?" He sounded skeptical.

"True," she conceded. "What else does that report have to say?"

"Among other things, that we can knock out the wall between the two small sitting rooms and make one large recreation area. The smaller room across the hall from this one, I want left as a study."

"Good, I'd love a study," Libby said aggressively.

"Two desks—we'll share," he countered. "Although how I'm supposed to concentrate on anything with your beautiful body sitting across from me . . ." His eyes homed in on her breasts, clearly outlined beneath her thin T-shirt. The hot glow in his eyes sent Libby's hopes for the rest of the day skyrocketing, and she followed him out into the kitchen on a rising tide of cautious happiness.

"The architect says that he could easily fit a half bath under the front stairway and he suggested putting a full bath in the kitchen where the pantry is now, if we decided to turn the whole back of the house into one huge kitchen."

"Good idea." She gingerly made her way over the ripped black linoleum. "That would let you clean up grubby kids before they tracked dirt through the rest of the house. What about putting in a set of French doors leading from the dining area to the backyard?"

"The architect suggested sliding glass doors since they're more energy efficient as well as being more secure. I'm inclined to agree. French doors would provide easy access for burglars."

"It's a shame we even have to consider that point." She grimaced.

"It's one of the prices you pay for living in the city. The trick is to take reasonable precautions while avoiding developing a siege mentality."

"I know." She admitted the truth of what he was saying. "At least sliding glass doors will let in lots of light."

"And make it easy to keep an eye on the kids playing in the yard."

"Hmm." Those kids he kept harping on were becoming very real to her.

"I was thinking of putting a large skylight about here." He looked up at the cracked plaster ceiling. "Right over where I'm going to put the cooking island."

Libby merely nodded, tacitly admitting that he was much better qualified to design a kitchen than she was, although she did like the idea of a skylight.

"What about the dining room?" She poked her head into the dark room.

"The architect suggested ripping out all that brown wainscoting. It's not authentic. It was added during the twenties. We can't enlarge the room because the wall between it and the kitchen is a bearing wall. It's where the original house ended. The kitchen and housekeeper's room were added right after the Civil War."

"Where did they cook before that?"

"The basement. And the servants were relegated to the unheated attic. Let's go up." He opened the door to the back stairwell.

"Ask your architect if he can do anything about the steepness of these stairs, will you?" Libby carefully made her way up as Joe scribbled in his notebook.

And this hall could certainly use brightening up."

"Maybe concealed lighting?" He continued to scribble.

Libby wandered into the master bedroom and glanced around consideringly. It was the only bedroom that wasn't small, and it was huge. It ran the entire back of the house.

"Mmm." Joe studied the dilapidated room. "We could easily put a walk-in closet on the north side. And a bath," he added. "I refuse to share a bathroom with a bunch of kids."

"What?" Libby looked at him in mock astonishment. "There's something about kids that you don't like?"

"After the hatchet job you and those young cousins of yours did on parenthood, there's lots I've found I don't like about kids."

"There's nothing like hands-on experience to clear up misconceptions, is there?" She grinned cheerfully at him. "Although actually I agree with your desire for a private bath. Where was the . . . ?" She paused and went back into the hall, opening the first door on the right.

"I thought I remembered the bathroom being there." She frowned up at the bare light bulb dangling from the ceiling. "I hope you know a good electrician because the lighting in this place is pure early Edison. To say nothing of the plumbing." She looked askance at the antique toilet.

"No problem." He glanced inside. "This may have been a small bedroom, but it makes a very large bath."

"Just a minute, I want to have a quick look at the rest of the rooms first." She worked her way down the hallway, opening and closing doors. She finished up in the tiny room directly across from the bath. She flipped on the light switch, shuddering when nothing happened.

"What's wrong?" Joe pushed open the heavy oak door to allow the faint glimmer from the hallway to provide a small amount of illumination.

"Someone's put dark contact paper over the window. I wonder why."

"Maybe they were into photography and used it as a darkroom."

"It's certainly that." Libby ventured farther into the small room, jumping when she stepped on a piece of paper that crackled beneath her foot.

"Lord!" She breathed deeply, then sneezed. "This is spooky."

"It's broad daylight."

"Not in here." She grimaced. "In here, it's kind of a perpetual twilight." A shiver chased over her skin. "I wonder if there are any ghosts."

"Ghosts?" he hooted. "Don't tell me an intellectual like you actually believes in the supernatural."

"The more man discovers, the more he realizes how much he doesn't know," she said seriously. "This house has been here for a long time, maybe . . . ."

"Augh!" Libby gasped as a pair of hard arms suddenly encircled her rib cage. "Joe Landowski, you frightened me out of my wits."

"Was it a short trip?" He laughed as his hands slipped up to cover her breasts, and he pulled her back into his hard chest. The firm globes absorbed the warmth from his hands, swelling to aching fullness. It felt so right to have him touch her. She inhaled deeply, an action that pressed her tingling flesh into his hands. Her mind was sinking in a warm well of desire. She made a determined effort to pull herself together.

"What . . . ?" She winced at the breathless quality of her voice, firmed it and continued, "What are you doing?"

"I am the ghost of houses past." Joe's deep voice rumbled in his chest.

"Really?" She giggled. "Tell me, are you exclusive to this house?"

"Just to the bedrooms." His fingers began to knead her breasts, and Libby arched into him, feeling as if a liquid fire

was shooting through her. "And I'm very particular abou
who I haunt."

"Peculiar, you said?"

"Particular, wench. I don't haunt just anybody." He gently
tugged at her hardening nipples through the thin material o
her T-shirt. She trembled as the delightful sensation fed he
growing passion.

"Oh?" The soft, yearning sound of her voice echoed dimly
in the small, empty room.

"You better believe it." He nuzzled her ear and Libby shuddered at the raspy texture of his chin, moving caressingly ove
her skin. His tongue darted out to stroke over the fine hai
on the back of her neck and she quivered in response.

"We ghosts have our standards. We can only be bothered
with sexy little morsels like you."

And Myrna and heaven knows how many others, the
thought suddenly surfaced. She might be responding to his
touch from the depths of her newly discovered love, but Joe
was responding on a much more elemental level. Oh, she
knew she appealed to him physically. He wouldn't have made
love to her unless he was attracted to her. But it was quite
possible that his feelings were founded on nothing more than
plain old-fashioned lust, that there was no difference in wha
he felt for her than in what he'd felt for Myrna. The unpalatable fact seeped through her body, extinguishing the flame
of her desire. She became tense in his embrace, and he sensed
it immediately.

"What's wrong, Libby?" Joe turned her around and smiled
tenderly down into her troubled eyes.

"I think the dust is beginning to get to me," she lied. She
could hardly tell him the truth. He might tolerate a lot of
idiosyncracies in his girlfriends, but having one fall in love
with him would be going much too far. And she didn't even
have the right to call herself a girlfriend, she thought, the
distressing truth intruding. Not really. He hadn't chosen her.
She was simply someone his father had wished on him.

"It is rather dusty in here." He glanced around in frustration. "But there's not much sense in trying to clean up with the builders due in next week."

"True. Let's just hurry a little." She grabbed at the excuse to cut short their planning session. She was finding it harder and harder to enter wholeheartedly into his plans for the simple reason that she desperately wanted them to be real. For him to be really remodeling this old house for a family. For their family. But her mind told her that it was much more likely that he had simply picked up the house as an investment and was weaving the remodeling of it into the game of their contract.

"Sure." Joe's arm remained companionably around her shoulder, and she used the excuse of inspecting the woodwork to escape. She found it hard to remember that she was a rational, logical adult when her body was pressed up against him.

"Now then." She took a deep breath and returned to the problem at hand. "We could make the present bath the master bath by putting a door through to the master bedroom and closing off the door in the hallway. Then turn the darkroom beside it into the kids' bath."

"Hmm. That would give us two baths up here."

"Plus one and a half downstairs."

"That should be plenty." He nodded. "And that still leaves six kids' room."

"No, it doesn't," she corrected him. "It leaves six cells that would be right at home in a monastery. You were the one who said that kids need room. Why don't you simply knock out connecting walls and make three good-sized bedrooms?"

"But then they'd have to share," he objected, following her as she wandered down the hall.

"Not if you only had three kids." She smiled sweetly at him.

"Only three?"

"It's fate. Three bedrooms, three kids."

"But we have six bedrooms."

"I told you they aren't bedrooms; they're cells."

"But I really wanted six kids," he repeated for at least th hundredth time.

"And I don't," Libby shot back.

Joe leaned against the filthy doorframe of the tiny corne bedroom and thoughtfully rubbed the bridge of his nose. "It' not what I really wanted. . . ."

"Welcome to the club. It's not what I really wanted, either I might remind you that that's the essence of compromise.

He took a deep breath as if steeling himself for the effor and said, "All right, I agree, but since I'm the one who's giv ing the most on this, how about if you give on education?"

"Give what?" she asked cautiously, rather surprised tha he'd actually accepted her compromise. Somehow she' never really expected him to relent an inch on the subject o family size. But then it wasn't real, she repeated again. Whe he finally decided to marry in earnest, he'd probably fin some semiliterate idiot who'd be willing to accept his sizabl income in exchange for being a baby factory. And she' probably turn the bedrooms back into cells. Libby felt an ag onizing flash of jealousy twist her stomach at the ver thought of some other woman living in this house and shar ing Joe's bed. For a brief second she fiercely wished that sh was more what he wanted in a wife. That she could be eve faintly happy staying at home and raising a brood of kids. Bu she wouldn't be. And trying to convince herself otherwis wouldn't work. She'd wind up resenting both Joe and the lov that had trapped her into a role that she wasn't suited for.

No, she sighed. Better to remember Joe and her love for hin with joy than to do something that would condemn that lov to a lingering death. A long, lingering death. He would neve agree to a divorce. When he married, it would truly be for life

"There's no reason to look so apprehensive." He misrea her expression. "All I'm asking is that you agree to send th kids to Catholic schools through high school."

"With one provision. New York City has some of the finest specialty high schools in the country. If we have a child who's gifted in one particular area, he should be able to go."

"If he wants to," he amended.

"All right." She nodded.

"Good, that's settled. I've got the contract over at my place. If you're through here, we can go back to my apartment and write up our compromise before you change your mind."

"Or you do," Libby corrected. "You're the one with the cast-iron view of everything."

"It only seems that way because I see more clearly."

"Yes, blinkers do tend to focus your vision on a rather narrow field."

"You're the one with tunnel vision," he countercharged. "You're so busy being fulfilled that you've missed the fact that first and foremost you're a woman."

"No. First, and foremost, I'm me. Libby Michalowski, a unique individual, and if I'm not true to myself, I can hardly be true to anyone else."

"I refuse to get into a pointless philosophical discussion. Let's go back to my place and write this up. Then we can send out for some pizza and write up our ideas for the house. I want to get this over to the architect tomorrow."

"Two pizzas." Libby happily fell in with his plans. "I'm starved."

"Man does not live by bread alone," he intoned, the sensual smile curving his mouth sitting oddly on his pious words.

"Oh? You mean he needs some television, too?" Libby teased as a warmth surged through her at his words. Apparently he intended to do more this evening than to merely talk. A course of action she heartily agreed with. Their association couldn't last all that much longer. At the rate they were revising the contract, they'd be finished in another couple of weeks. Definitely by the end of August and once the contract was done, they'd have no reason to see each other again.

The awful thought filled her mind and made her all the mor
determined to store up as many memories as possible for th
long, lonely years that loomed ahead of her.

"Don't mention television!" Joe shuddered. "I'm still hav
ing nightmares about *The Hobbit*."

Libby studied the rueful smile on his face and a wave o
tenderness caught her unaware. Oh, but she loved him
Loved his intelligent mind, his even temperament, his un
failing good humor, the funny way he tipped his head to on
side when he was thinking. She loved everything about him
Letting him go when the contract was finished would tear he
heart out. But trying to keep him would do the same thing.

"Joe Landowski, you are one helluva nice man." Her word
had the reverence of a vow, and his eyes took on a deeper hu
as he studied her features.

"And you, Libby Michalowski, are a woman of rare an
redeeming value. Now let's go home and explore those two
ideas in depth." He held out his large hand and Libby put her
in his, shivering as his long fingers closed over hers. She had
the fanciful notion that he'd just claimed much more than he
hand.

12

"HELLO, LIBBY. Joe here." Libby grimaced. Of all the super-fluous statements she'd ever heard, that had to top the list. She'd recognize that deep-brown-velvet voice anywhere. All it took was one word and her entire nervous system went on red alert.

"Sorry to bother you at dinnertime, but it's the third Thursday of the month."

"That's probably because yesterday was the third Wednesday." She made an effort to respond naturally though intense pleasure at simply hearing his voice swamped her. This was awful. She was becoming more susceptible to him with every additional exposure. And there'd been lots of ad-ditional exposure, she thought wryly. Over the past week and a half, Joe had seemed to be constantly in her company. Oc-casionally he'd had a specific reason having to do with the contract, but more often than not he'd simply appeared on her doorstep with plans for the evening. Plans that she'd weakly gone along with. In the back of her mind, she knew that indulging in her compulsive desire to be with him was going to cause her a lot of heartache in the future when the contract was completed and the charade ended, but she still wasn't strong enough to turn down his invitations. Instead she had hoarded each one, greedily distilling the last ounce of pleasure from it. At times she had even allowed herself to pretend that he loved her. That what he felt for her was more than warm friendship, enhanced by an almost perfect phys-ical relationship.

"Libby!" Joe's voice sliced into her thoughts and she hastily returned to earth.

"Sorry. I've been grading a test that I gave today and my mind feels like mush," she told him, which was only part of the truth.

"I do a great massage."

"It sounds messy."

"It couldn't be. I'm positive that you're as beautiful inside as you are out."

"Fie, and aren't you the flatterer, sir." Love warmed her voice. "With a line like that you'll go far."

"Think so?"

"Go far before you manage to find a woman desperate enough to swallow it."

"No, no. You've got it all wrong. Women are supposed to stroke the male ego. Not deflate it."

"Personally I prefer to stroke something a little more substantial than your ego."

"Oh?" His husky whisper shortened her breath. "If I didn't have a meeting tonight, I'd come over and we could explore your statement in depth. I know how into research you academic types are."

"Not when the results are a foregone conclusion," she teased, hiding her disappointment that she wouldn't be seeing him tonight.

"I called you primarily because I got the contract back today."

"Did they add anything?" she asked.

"Only catsup stains. They must be doing their editing at a restaurant. I think we're going to have to find them a useful occupation." He chuckled.

"They already have one. Marrying us off."

"For the time being," he replied cryptically, plunging her into a maelstrom of uncertainty. Could he possibly mean that he was going to fulfill their fathers' fondest wishes and marry her? A wave of joy flooded her only to retreat in the face of common sense. Their fathers might have actually gotten him thinking about marriage and a family, but that was no reason to assume that Joe had cast her in the role of his wife. Even if by some miracle he had, she wasn't certain she really wanted to marry a male chauvinist.

"Libby," he said exasperatedly, "long silences in phone conversations are very disconcerting."

"Sorry, you were saying . . . ?"

"That we need to go over the contract."

"Well, we can't tonight because you've got a meeting. How about tomorrow, or do you want to wait till the weekend?" Libby was careful not to sound too eager. Her pride demanded that he understand she wasn't trying to make any claims on him.

"That brings me to the second reason I called. My plans have been finalized."

"Plans?" she asked forebodingly.

"Mmm. A business trip. I have to go to Europe for the semiannual fabric shows."

"Europe!" she gasped.

"I'll be gone for two weeks and I want you to go with me."

"Go with you?" she repeated dumbly.

"Yes, go with me. You've got a passport, haven't you?"

"Of course, but I can't just drop everything and fly off into the blue."

"Why not?"

"Why not? What am I supposed to do about my classes?"

"Get a substitute. They'd survive if you got sick."

"That's not the point." Libby kept her voice level with an effort. She was torn by conflicting emotions. Part of her wanted to do just as he'd suggested. To forget everything and go with him. And yet part of her was furious that he attached so little importance to her job.

"Then what is the point?" His voice had an edge to it.

"That I signed a contract to teach. These aren't grade-school classes that just any competent adult could handle.

These are graduate-level math classes. Substitutes are few and far between, especially in the summer. It would be grossly unfair to my students to suddenly take off for two weeks."

"And what about being unfair to me?" he said tightly.

"What about you?" Her voice rose in anger at the choice he was forcing on her. "You had to know that this trip was in the offing and yet you sprang it on me at the last minute."

"It was supposed to be a surprise."

"Well, congratulations! It was."

"You won't go?" he bit out.

"I can't go," Libby said through clenched teeth. "Listen to what I'm saying. I have a responsibility to my students as well as to the university. A legal as well as a moral obligation that I willingly accepted. I can't suddenly fling it over and leave them to fend for themselves because something better came along."

"If it were all that much better, you would."

"Would you ignore your responsibilities?"

"That's different. I'm a man."

"A pigheaded man mired in double standards!" Libby yelled into the phone. "Why the hell should there be one set of rules for you and a different set for me?"

"It has nothing to do with a double standard!" he thundered, but in her own fury Libby didn't even register her eardrum's protest. "It has to do with that damned job of yours. If you weren't working, you could come."

"If I weren't working, I'd be living at home with my folks, and if I were doing that, I could hardly take off with some man for two weeks, now could I?" she gibed.

"I'm not some man!" Joe roared. "And I'm also not going to stand for your putting your job before me." There was an ominous silence as if he was waiting for her capitulation, but she was too angry to notice.

"Then try sitting down for it!" she yelled, slamming down the phone, and promptly burst into tears, which further infuriated her. She never cried, and that she should be doing so now, over some egocentric male chauvinist, was galling.

"Run off to Europe indeed!" she sputtered angrily. How could he possibly expect her to simply let everyone down just to please herself? And it would please her, she admitted honestly. The very idea of spending two weeks traveling with Joe was exhilarating. Equally elating was the fact that he actually wanted her to accompany him. Or did he always take a woman along on these trips? Had Myrna traveled with him? The unpalatable thought made her tears flow all the harder.

Twenty minutes later, Libby made a determined effort to get a grip on herself. Crying wasn't helping. It was only giving her a headache and making her look a mess. She winced at the sight of her red, swollen eyes, blotchy complexion and bright pink nose.

He wasn't worth it, she told herself, and then sniffed disconsolately at the blatant untruth. He really was. Except for his archaic ideas about his wife's role in life, Joe Landowski was everything that a woman could want in a man. He had a depth to his character that she could spend the rest of her life plumbing. But she wasn't going to get the chance, she acknowledged as the tears began to trickle down her cheeks again. After her emphatic refusal to fall in with his plans, he'd undoubtedly take great pains never to see her again, contract or no contract. The thought turned the trickle into a flood and she leaned back, giving way to her despair. It wasn't like her, but neither had the choice he'd forced on her been normal. To have had to choose between her desire to please the man she loved and her responsibility had been a devastating experience.

At last her tears slowed and then stopped, but Libby continued to sit on the couch, too sunk in misery to move. Finally her self-respect routed the self-pity she was wallowing in. She firmed her lips and poured herself a drink of straight whisky. She gulped it down, ignoring the way it burned a fiery path to her stomach. Then she wiped the drying tears off her cheeks with the back of her hand, defiantly blew her nose and reached for the tests she'd been grading.

But it quickly became apparent that it was an exercise in futility. Her eyes felt full of sand, her nose was clogged and her head was throbbing so badly, she found it impossible to concentrate on the intricate math problems. But she refused to quit. It was bad enough that he was destroying her emotionally, she wasn't going to allow him to mess up her professional life.

Half an hour later the doorbell rang. Libby put down her red pencil and wearily rubbed her forehead, ignoring the summons. She didn't want to see anyone. Not ever again. A self-pitying sniff broke through the rigid self-control she was struggling to maintain. But whoever was there refused to take no for an answer. Whoever it was depressed the bell and the continued buzzing was rapidly escalating her headache into the realm of excruciating torment. Finally she could stand it no longer and with a muffled curse she marched to the door and flung it open.

Her eyes widened at the sight of Joe. His hair was rumpled as if he'd been running agitated fingers through it, his wine-colored tie had been tugged loose and the top button on his white shirt was undone. His gray vest was hanging open and his suit jacket was clutched in one of his large hands.

The sight of his beloved face intensified her unhappiness and she started to slam the door shut. But he was too quick for her. He grabbed the door, pushed it open and moved into the apartment, forcing her backward.

"High-handed male," she accused halfheartedly, feeling too miserable to get angry at the way he'd barged in.

"What do you want?" She watched him fling his exquisitely tailored suit jacket on the couch.

"You!" He grabbed her and yanked her up against him.

Her body was firmly pressed along his muscular length, and his warm, musky scent flooded her muddled senses.

Libby sniffed unhappily. She loved him so much. She couldn't bear to fight with him again.

"I've already told you. I can't go. No matter what my personal feelings, I have to honor my commitments."

"Would you rather go with me than teach?" His eyes narrowed as he studied her pale, unhappy face.

"Certainly," she admitted. "No matter how much I love teaching there's bound to be times when it's a nuisance." She tried to step back, but his grip on her tightened and he suddenly swept her up into his arms and strode toward her bedroom.

"What are you doing?" she demanded.

"Applying the time-honored solution to this fight." He elbowed open the door, strode across the pale blue carpet and dropped her onto the blue flowered satin quilt.

Libby peered up at him through swollen eyes, her breath quickening as he ripped off his tie, shrugged out of his vest and unbuttoned his shirt. Hungrily she watched the muscles on his broad chest ripple as he tugged the shirt free and dropped it on the floor.

This was a bad idea. Her mind screamed the information, but Libby turned the volume down. She didn't really need the reminder that making love wasn't going to solve any of the underlying problems. If anything, their lovemaking was a hindrance because it tended to obscure their differences. But none of that really mattered. What mattered was that she loved him as she had never loved anyone before or, she very much feared, would ever love any one in the future, and she wanted to express that love in the most basic way possible.

Her eyes drifted shut as his hand went to his belt buckle. She heard the sound of his zipper opening, followed by the two thumps his discarded shoes made as they hit the floor. She scooted over as he sat down beside her hips. Blindly she reached for him. Her fingers seemed to momentarily stick as she touched his burning skin, and then her hands burrowed beneath the thick pelt of golden blond hair that covered his chest. She flexed her fingers, gently digging her nails into his supple skin. He tensed slightly at her action and a small, satisfied smile teased her lips as she deliberately emptied her mind of everything but Joe.

She reveled in the feel of his soft skin, of the crisp abrasiveness of his body hair, of the rigid line of his collarbone as her fingers slowly explored it. She delved into the deep V at the base of his neck before drifting lower to discover his nipples. Her nails flicked them and Libby felt him tremble, fiercely glad that he was as responsive to her touch as she was to his. Or was it simply that he was responsive to a woman's touch? Any woman's? The question bubbled to the surface of her mind only to dissolve in her erupting passion as Joe's hands slid beneath her knit skirt. His long fingers splayed across her slender rib cage, their tips just barely pressing against the soft swell of her breasts.

His hard flesh was warm on her skin and she could feel the now familiar heat beginning to grow deep in her loins. An intense quiver shook the very heart of her femininity and she trembled convulsively. Her emotions had taken such a beating this evening that she seemed to have no control over them. They were entirely open to him and what he was doing.

"My precious Libby, you feel so perfect." His husky voice sent shivers down her spine. Slowly his hands crept upward under her shirt to finally cover the soft globes of her breasts.

She licked her dry lips and tried to steady her erratic breathing. A task that became impossible as he slowly rotated his palms over the tight buds. Back and forth he moved while she began to shake with the force of the desire tearing through her. She clutched his shoulders and tugged him toward her. She needed him. Needed him to heal the scars of their fight.

"What do you want, Libby?" His voice was rough with the strength of his burgeoning passion. "Do you crave me a tenth as much as I do you?" His mouth suddenly captured hers, urging her lips open. His tongue plunged inside, stroking aggressively over her velvety moistness. A paroxysm of sensation thundered in her ears and pounded through her veins. Long before she'd drunk her fill of the taste of his mouth, he withdrew.

"Joe," Libby protested the loss. Her tongue explored her swollen, throbbing lips, and then slowly her eyes opened. She stared up at him through the fog of her ardor.

His face seemed a collection of sharp angles and hard planes. The force of his passion was clearly stamped on his features. His eyes seemed to glow with tiny lights burning deep within their velvety depths.

She waited in breathless anticipation as slowly, much too slowly, he pulled the hem of her top upward until at last her breasts were free. The cool air of the bedroom wafted over them a second before Joe reverently cupped each one. His thumbs grazed the sensitive tips and a smile of sensual satisfaction curved his lips.

"You feel so fragile." His wondering voice tightened the coil of her need. "Soft and ethereal, like a dream that's haunted me for years. You make me forget everything but the reality of you beneath me." He swooped, capturing one dusky-pink nipple. Lightly he held it captive with his strong white teeth while he caressed it with the tip of his moist tongue.

"Joe!" Libby frantically clutched his head, shuddering under the onslaught of sensation. Not satisfied, he began to tug at the tip of her other breast with his thumb and forefinger. Inarticulate sounds of frustrated pleasure escaped her, and she arched her body into his devouring mouth. Tremors convulsed her abdomen and a dampening heat grew deep within her.

Her breath whistled through her lungs as his mouth moved, trailing downward over her rib cage. She quivered as he parted her legs, his large hands moving up under her denim skirt, tracing intricate patterns on the silken skin of her inner thighs.

Libby waited, every muscle locked in breathless anticipation, as his hand climbed higher and higher until it brushed
slowly over the sleekness of her panties. She dug her feet into
the bed and arched her body into the heel of his hand as a
convulsive shudder racked her body.

"Oh, yes!" she gasped.

"Definitely, my precious one." His voice was gruff and his
hands were unsteady as he gently tugged her panties down
over her slender legs and tossed them aside.

Libby flung her arms around his waist and tried to pull him
to her. He resisted for a fraction of a second, continuing to
explore her moist feminine warmth. Just when she thought
she'd scream with frustration, he surged forward and Libby
triumphed in the masculine invasion, holding him close as if
trying to absorb him into her bloodstream.

I love you, Joe Landowski, her mind silently vowed while
her breathing came in short, staccato gasps. Too soon, much
too soon, when all she wanted to do was to savor the moment forever, the tight coil within her snapped, dropping her
into an exploding kaleidoscope of pure ecstasy. She could feel
the stiffening of Joe's muscles as he followed her, and she tenderly held him, never wanting to let him go, when he finally
lay sprawled across her sated body.

He shifted onto his side and pulled her limp form up against
his sweat-dampened chest. Libby nestled her face against his
shoulder and a sigh of pure happiness escaped her.

"Darling, Libby." Joe smoothed her tangled hair back from
her flushed face. "I'm sorry."

She froze in horror. He was sorry! They'd just shared the
most perfect experience of her life and he felt it necessary to
apologize. Before she could give voice to the dismay chilling
her, he continued.

"It was unreasonable of me to expect you to drop everything on a moment's notice and leave the country with me.
My only excuse is that I was extremely hurt when you refused to go. I'd been planning all the things I wanted to show

you on our trip, and when you said no I reacted out of the depths of my own disappointment." The sincerity of his voice was unmistakable.

"That's all right," she murmured, rather surprised he was being so open about what he had felt. And why had he been so disappointed anyway? Was it possible that he thought of her as more than a friend? But how was she to find out, she wondered and then admitted that she couldn't. Asking would reveal her own love. If it wasn't reciprocated, and there was no reason to assume that it was, it would undoubtedly spell the end of their relationship.

"I guess it's time I faced up to the fact that neither logic, yelling, nor plain old begging is going to change your mind about your job, is it?" he continued in resignation.

"My teaching is part of me."

"So we're left with the question of how to best reconcile my wanting a full-time wife and mother for our children with your holding down a job."

"Well..." Libby was willing to give a little now that he'd finally admitted she had a right to a career in addition to motherhood. "I could give up teaching summer school. I don't always do it anyway and that would give me two and a half months free a year."

"All right. And I'll try whenever possible to schedule overseas business trips in the summer so that you can accompany me. But what about the kids? Young children need their mother."

"Wrong. Young children need their parents."

"Not in the beginning," he argued. "I can't nurse them."

"We've already settled that," she insisted. "And anyway they're infants for such a very short time."

"But it's a crucial time in their development."

Libby sighed, fearing that he was right. "I'm allowed to take a year's maternity leave with each child. That should certainly be enough time to get them off to a good start."

"Maybe." He sounded doubtful, but resigned. "And I could arrange to work at home a couple of afternoons a week so at least I'd be there."

"Don't underestimate yourself," she teased. "You're as good as most mothers I've seen."

"Flattery will get you anywhere." He leered happily at her.

"Anywhere?" She batted her eyelashes and tried to look innocent. A difficult task when she was lying naked in his arms.

"We've already been there, wench."

"Ah, but the old favorites are always best." She traced his jawline with a questioning fingertip.

"You could be right." He rolled over, pulling her up onto his broad chest.

She gasped as the feel of his muscular body began to re-kindle her passion. "Mmm." She wiggled into his contours, glorying in his growing reaction to her.

"Just a minute, Libby." His arms held her still. "I want to make sure I've got this right, to put it in the contract. You agree to give up summer school and to take a year's mater-nity leave with each child?"

"Right." She nodded. "And in exchange you agree to work at home two afternoons a week."

"It's a deal." Joe sighed. "But I'd still rather have you at home all the time."

"That's the last complaint you get," she said seriously. "Once you agree to something, you can't be constantly la-menting what you didn't get."

"Fair enough, but I can get what I really want right now." His eyes began to gleam as he pulled her body upward along the length of his hard frame.

"What we both want," Libby corrected, melting into him.

13

HE'S HOME, HE'S HOME, he's home! The words rang in Libby's mind like a joyful litany. After two interminable weeks, Joe was actually home. In his apartment. Right this minute. She grinned idiotically as the driver of the school bus stopped in traffic beside her taxi. She felt as if she belonged in a musical. The kind where people burst into joyous song at the drop of a hat.

It seemed like years since Joe had left for Europe. She'd known she was going to miss him, but she'd drastically underestimated just how much. As she'd underestimated many things. Such as how much the possibility that he might suddenly appear on her doorstep would add a sense of excitement to her daily routine. How strong was her habit of saving happenings from her classes to share with him. How much she looked forward to hearing about the events that had filled his day. How much she enjoyed simply being with him.

Even his nightly phone calls hadn't alleviated her longing to see him. To touch him. She'd been too conscious of how much the calls were costing, and faintly appalled by how her heart had leaped at the sound of his voice, to be completely natural with him. But all that was over. Excitement spiraled through her. The interminable two weeks had finally passed. He was back. He'd called her from the airport an hour ago, telling her he'd managed to get an earlier flight and asking her to meet him at his apartment. She sighed nervously. She craved seeing Joe so intensely that she wondered if, perhaps, she hadn't exaggerated his importance in her mind. If seeing him wouldn't turn out to be an anticlimax.

Two hours later, she knew that if anything, she'd minimized her longing to see him. And she was almost able to believe that he'd missed her with an equal fervor. His welcoming kiss had flared out of control, and they'd made love with an intensity that had brought joyous tears to her eyes.

"Thank you, my darling Libby." Joe kissed the top of her head, which was snuggled against his shoulder. "I've been fantasizing about making love to you for two long weeks, but not even my imagination could compare to the reality."

"Mmm," she purred, finding it hard to surface from the languor that had followed their cataclysmic lovemaking.

"Up, Libby."

"How can you sound so alert? Aren't you supposed to have jet lag or something?"

"Not coming back. I gained five hours. So up you go. We've got to get dressed."

"Why?" She yawned and stretched, shivering slightly as his warm fingers began to idly trace the curve of her spine.

"Because I'm hungry."

"So am I." She giggled, running a caressing finger over his flat belly.

"Not that kind of hunger, wench!" He tipped her off his chest onto the mattress of his king-size bed and stood up. "I haven't had anything to eat since supper last night."

"And you're wasting away to nothing." She feasted her eyes on the magnificent lines of his body.

"Where's your maternal streak? You're supposed to want to feed me," he complained.

"Wrong generation. It's my mother who believes food cures all ills. But I will fix you something," she offered, perfectly willing to cook the meal since she could leave him with the dirty dishes.

"Ha!" He turned from his dresser where he was rummaging through the top drawer. "You expect me to trust my stomach to a woman who gets her cakes out of a box?"

"Better than getting them out of a rum bottle!"

"You, madam, have very plebeian taste buds."

"I must. I like you." She grinned. He looked so ridiculous standing there wearing a haughty expression and nothing else.

"Your lack of cooking skill is no laughing matter," he insisted. "I'll take you out to dinner."

"Fine. I'll use the shower in the guest room." She gathered up her clothes, which were scattered around the room, flushing slightly at the impetuous way she'd discarded them.

"The final version of the contract's in the living room on the coffee table. Dad dropped it off while I was gone. You can go over it when you're through. I need to check with my secretary before we go."

Libby rushed through her shower, anxious not to waste a precious second of her time with Joe. As a result, when she arrived in the living room, he hadn't finished his phone call. So she picked up the completed contract and began to read it. Despite the fact that this whole affair had begun simply as an exercise in circumventing their fathers, what had finally emerged was a very real, workable blueprint for a relationship between two strong-minded personalities with widely differing views on family and marriage. It wasn't ideal as far as she was concerned, but she could live with it. Could Joe? She remembered the vehemence with which he had argued some points. "Finished?" he asked, and she jumped. She hadn't heard him approaching.

"Uh-huh." She handed him the contract. "Everything fine at the office?"

"More or less. Nothing that can't wait till tomorrow." Joe sank down on the sofa beside her, propped his feet up on the coffee table, and started to read the document.

"I see they've resisted the impulse to add anything." His eyes had a devilish twinkle as he reached the end. "Our fathers wanted a traditional approach to marriage. I'll add the most traditional touch of all." He picked up the gold pen laying on the coffee table and scribbled something under his signature.

"What touch is that?" Libby asked idly, her attention centered on the way the muscles of his forearm rippled as he wrote.

"A virgin bride, of course," he said, chuckling.

A virgin bride. *A virgin bride!* The incredible words beat through her mind, gaining volume as they ricocheted. All of her earlier doubts about the wisdom of going to bed with him returned to haunt her. Why, oh why, hadn't she listened to her instincts, she thought despairingly. He'd dropped enough clues that a blind woman could have figured it out, but had she? Oh, no. She'd ignored what her mind was telling her and followed her heart, and where had it gotten her? Dismissed to the wrong side of the pale. Even if he had been considering marriage, her precipitous action had removed her from the running, she acknowledged desolately. By accepting him as her lover, she'd forfeited the right to be his wife.

Suddenly anger began to dissolve away her misery. Who the hell did Joe Landowski think he was, dividing women into acceptable and unacceptable strictly on the basis of sexual experience!

She jumped to her feet and glared down into his startled face. A hectic flush stained her pale cheeks and sparks of fury lit the luminescent depths of her blue eyes.

"What's wrong?"

"You!" Libby gritted out. "Or, more specifically, your double standard."

"Double standard?"

"How dare you demand something you can't deliver yourself! Of all the sanctimonious, hypocritical bastards!" she yelled at him. "Demanding a bride as pure as the driven snow when you've got the morals of an alley cat!"

"Oh now . . ." he began, but she chopped him off.

"Don't you talk to me you . . . you . . . degenerate playboy! I hope when you finally find yourself some naive little virgin, she has the same standards you do and tells you she won't stoop to marry some promiscuous rake!"

"I am not promiscuous!"

"It applies to males as well as females, Joe Landowski."

"What the hell are you so mad about?" he demanded, his features hardening against her vehement attack.

"Figure it out, bright boy!" Libby screamed at him. "You're the one who likes a challenge." She grabbed her purse off the end table and stalked toward the door.

"Where are you going?" He grabbed for her, but she danced out of reach. "We haven't had dinner."

"I feel nauseous," she said in perfect truth. She was so angry her stomach was churning wildly. "Besides, I wouldn't want to contaminate you."

"Would you quit talking in riddles and give me a straight answer?"

"All right." She clenched her teeth and took a deep breath. "I'll tell you what's the matter. I deeply resent the fact that you feel I'm good enough for a brief tumble in the hay, but socially unacceptable when it comes to being a wife."

"Socially unacceptable?" He looked confused.

"Damn you, I'm not a virgin!" She jerked open the front door, missing the horrified consternation that spread over his face. Her entire attention was focused on her own anger and hurt. She sprinted for the elevator, ignoring his shouted command to wait. She couldn't face him and, besides, there was no point. All she wanted to do was go home and hide. She felt as if the bottom had suddenly dropped out of her world.

You fool, she castigated herself as the elevator carried her farther away from Joe. You knew what he was like and yet you convinced yourself that you would be the exception. She swallowed a sob. She wasn't going to cry over him. She wasn't! He wasn't worth it. She was better off without him, but the trouble was that she didn't believe it. Despite everything, she still loved him and she had the devastating feeling that she always would.

"WELL, FREDERIC," Casimir said, sliding into a chair, "what was so important that we had to meet immediately?"

"Yes?" Sigismund glanced up. "What's happened? The contract seemed to have been worked out down to the last detail."

"I'm not sure." Frederic's faded blue eyes held a deep puzzlement. "All I know for certain is that Joe called me last night and said that he needed help."

"Help?" Casimir looked dumbfounded.

"Yes, help. He said since it was all our fault, we could figure out what to do. I think the last time he asked for help he was six and had tangled his kite in a tree," he mused.

"Has Libby said anything?" Casimir turned to Sigismund.

"No." He paused thoughtfully. "She seemed kind of restless while Joe was out of the country, but I haven't seen her since he came back and that was almost a week ago."

"All our fault," Casimir reflected. "I wonder why we're to blame now. If he were going to have gotten mad, the time to have done it was when we started, not when we've finished."

"You can ask him yourself. Here he comes now." Frederic nodded to where Joe was making his way across the almost empty restaurant. His lips were firmly pressed together and his eyes seemed dulled with a despair that was reflected in his set features.

"Hi, Dad."

"Son. This is Casimir Blinkle and Sigismund Michalowski."

"Gentlemen." Joe shook hands and then sat in the remaining empty chair, seemingly at a loss over how to start.

"You wanted to see us?" Frederic prompted.

"Not really." Joe ran agitated fingers through his rumpled hair. "But you're my last resort. I've tried everything else."

"Unfortunately we lack a frame of reference from which to make any sense out of these obscure mutterings of yours," Casimir pointed out.

"Sorry." Joe sighed. "I haven't been sleeping well lately. The problem is Libby. We had a fight and, every time I call her to try to apologize, she hangs up. I can't get to her."

"Is it necessary that you do?" Frederic asked blandly.

"Yes." Joe sounded harassed. "You read the contract. You have to know that . . ."

"That your father managed to find you the perfect wife?" Frederic smiled smugly.

"Yes, dammit!" Joe snapped. "It should be obvious that I love her. I let her talk me out of everything I'd originally thought was absolutely essential in a marriage. Now I know that the only thing that's essential is Libby."

"So tell her," Sigismund suggested.

"I can't. I told you, she won't talk to me. I even resorted to calling that friend of hers, Jessie Anders. She told me I was lucky that Libby didn't put a contract out on me and then hung up."

"We were the last choice, weren't we?" Casimir said dryly.

"Suppose you tell us what went wrong?" Sigismund suggested.

"I did. We had a fight."

"But what about?" Frederic persisted.

"Never mind the details." Joe refused to elaborate. "Just take my word for it that I hurt her. I didn't mean to, but that doesn't alter the fact that I did."

"Really, Joseph," Frederic snapped, "I would have thought that a man with your vast experience with gorgeous women would have had more address than that."

"Libby's not a gorgeous woman," Joe stated emphatically.

"My daughter is an exceptionally gorgeous woman!" Sigismund glared at him.

"I know that! All I meant was that Libby isn't simply a gorgeous woman. She's a whole lot more. She's intelligent, warm, caring. She's got a fantastic sense of humor and she's—" He suddenly broke off and took a gulp of the whisky his father pushed toward him.

"Sexy? Desirable?" Sigismund finished for him and turned to Frederic. "Really, this younger generation is so mealymouthed."

"If you three are finished taking cheap shots at me, do you suppose we could get back to our problem?" Joe held on to his temper with a visible effort.

"Your problem," Frederic corrected. "You're the one who blew it."

"Yours, too, Dad, if you ever expect to have any grandchildren. If I can't marry Libby, then I won't marry anyone."

"Don't worry, my boy," Sigismund said. "Of course, we'll help you. Didn't we set it all up in the first place?"

"I considered that—" Joe gave him a threatening glance "—and I decided to come to you anyway. What I want you to do, Professor Michalowski, is ask Libby up to your apartment, where I'll be waiting for her."

"And what's to keep her from simply walking out again?" Sigismund asked.

"True," Casimir said, nodding. "You can hardly lock her in."

"No?" Joe's eyes began to gleam.

"No!" Casimir repeated emphatically. "All that would prove is that you're stronger than she is. Take my word for it, boy, using brute strength to win an argument is self-defeating."

"But I don't want to win it," Joe protested. "All I want to do is tell her how sorry I am."

"Well, locking her in the apartment is going to make her mad all over again."

"Then what am I supposed to do?" Joe demanded. "If I could just talk to her..."

"Yes." Sigismund rubbed his thin cheek. "And you need to do it in a situation where she'd be extremely hesitant to cause a scene."

"Such as?" Joe prompted eagerly.

"Such as my great-niece's baptism. Even Libby would think twice before losing her temper in church."

"You don't know how angry she was," Joe said gloomily.

"What we'll do," Sigismund continued undaunted, "is this. My wife and I were going by ourselves, but I'll call Libby and tell her that her mother isn't feeling well and she should come instead."

"Do you think she will?" Joe asked dubiously.

"Of course. I'm her father. If I ask her to come, she'll come. When we're seated, I'll say I left something in the car and leave. Then you can slip into the pew beside her. That'll give you the whole service to apologize, and if you can't accomplish it in an hour, then I wash my hands of you."

"I'll do it." Joe grabbed at the plan.

LIBBY SANK DOWN onto the hard wooden pew and glanced around her. The front of the church was filled with people she'd known most of her life, all of them here to celebrate the baptism of her cousin Sarah's new daughter. Libby suppressed a sigh. She'd never felt less like celebrating in her life. Her eyes felt as if they were full of sand, her stomach was a churning mass of nerves and her head was consumed by a dull ache. She couldn't sleep, she couldn't eat and pretty soon she wouldn't be able to teach. For the first time in her life, she failed to find any comfort in her beloved math. It had become a jumble of incomprehensible abstractions.

Without Joe, nothing in her life had any reality. She felt as if someone had torn the center out of her existence. She kept telling herself that she'd get over it, that no one ever died of a broken heart and she wouldn't be the first, but it did no good. The pain was as intense now as it had been a week ago when they'd had the fight. So great was her unhappiness that she'd finally decided to talk to him, but then he hadn't called again. It had been three days since he'd last tried to reach her, and she was left to the devastating conclusion that he'd found consolation elsewhere.

She swallowed a sob. *Don't you dare cry about that louse and his double standard*, she ordered herself. *Especially not here.* She noticed an elderly aunt, nodding benignly at her. Libby forced a smile. She hadn't wanted to come to the baptism, but now that she was here, good manners dictated that she not cast a shadow on the happy proceedings.

"Libby?" Her father's gentle hand on her shoulder caught her attention. "I forgot something in the car."

"I'll get it for you."

"No!" Sigismund said sharply, and then smiled at her look of surprise. "I won't be a minute. Save my place."

"Certainly." She sank back against the pew and closed her eyes. She was so tired. If only she could sleep. She felt her father slip back into the seat beside her, but she kept her eyes firmly shut. She didn't want to talk.

Slowly, very slowly, her body began to relax as the peace of the old church stole over her. But her hard-won serenity was shattered as her mind began to play cruel tricks on her. She could smell the elusive tang of Joe's after-shave. It trickled into her lungs and rasped over her raw emotions. She couldn't stand it anymore.

She turned to tell her father that she'd wait for him in the car and found herself staring into Joe's haggard face. Hungrily she drank in the sight of him, hoarding the precious image.

"Hello, Libby," he whispered.

His casual greeting brought her to her senses. How dare he act like nothing had happened? Righteous anger began to drift through the apathetic despair that held her captive. And her father. He had to have been a part to this. It was much too pat to be a coincidence.

"Don't you hello me, you male chauvinist!" Libby hissed, ignoring the shocked expression on her elderly aunt's face.

"Libby, I didn't mean it. I . . ." He paused as the organ began to play, filling the church with the sound of the processional.

Libby glanced behind her in frustration. The priests were walking down the aisle, so even if she did manage to push past Joe, she still couldn't leave.

"Yes you did," she whispered once the priests had passed them. "What you're sorry about is that I caught on and ended the charade before you could do it yourself." She stared at the altar, not even seeing the priest's actions.

"Listen to me." Joe grabbed her arm.

"I did," she sniffed. "And let go of my arm." She tried to break free of his hold, but couldn't do it without causing a scene. An unthinkable thing to do in church. They were already attracting unwelcome attention. She smiled sheepishly at the two elderly cousins who were gaping at them from across the aisle.

"Please, Libby," he gritted out.

"Why should I?" She glared at him.

"Because I love you, you stubborn—" he shouted, and then broke off in horror as he realized what he'd just done. A dull red tide stained his cheeks as the entire congregation turned to stare at them.

Libby gulped, frozen between embarrassed consternation and burgeoning hope. Before she could decided what to do, the priest, a distant relative of hers, solved her dilemma.

"Your feelings do you credit, young man. God knows, there's little enough love in the world. However, might I suggest that you and Libby retire to the outer vestibule to settle your differences and allow us to continue without any further interruptions?"

"Certainly, Father," Joe mumbled, stepping into the aisle and yanking Libby out with him.

She kept her eyes firmly fixed on the gray slate floor as she went, barely registering the interested murmurs that followed them. She was much more concerned with what Joe had said. If he'd actually meant it. She glowed with sudden hope. He'd never said that he loved her before. Not even when they'd been making love. He'd said that he liked her. That he admired her. That he wanted her. But never that illusive phrase that she'd given up hope of hearing.

Joe shouldered open the massive oak doors, pulled her through and let them close.

Libby glanced around the huge shadowy vestibule. It appeared to be empty. She stopped dead, refusing to move.

"At least do me the courtesy of listening to me!" he protested.

"I will, but right here. I'm not going anywhere with you until I hear your explanation."

He hunched his shoulders and turned his back to her, trailing his fingers through the font of holy water beside the door.

A feeling of tenderness shook her at his uncertain demeanor. He was nervous. He was actually afraid of her reaction. Ruthlessly she squelched the feeling. They had to solve this without clouding the issue with emotion.

"Libby." He swung back to her, his face set and his body held in rigid lines. "I didn't mean to hurt you. You have to believe that. I never thought of what I was saying as applying to you. I was just kidding around. I couldn't believe it when you took it personally."

"How did you expect me to take it?"

"I don't know," he said flatly. "It wasn't premeditated. It was one of those offhand things you say. Libby—" his fingers began to gently trace the line of her jaw "—I love you and you love me. Don't condemn us both to a lonely future simply because I hurt your pride."

"How do you know that I love you?" she muttered, the caressing movement of his hand confusing her exhausted mind.

"Because of the completeness with which you gave yourself to me." His eyes glowed with remembered pleasure. His hand left her cheek and captured her nape. His thumb slipped under her chin, forcing it upward and she found herself staring into his incandescent blue eyes. "Be generous enough to tell me the truth."

"All right." She sighed. "I do love you, aggravating man that you are. I don't know how or why, but I do. Oh, Joe, I've been so unhappy." Her voice wobbled and he pulled her into his arms. The scent of his cologne filled her nostrils while the heat from his large body encompassed her in a protective zone.

She sighed rapturously and snuggled her face into his crisp white collar. After her despair of the past week, it seemed too much to suddenly comprehend that he loved her.

"When can we be married?" Joe demanded.

"Married?"

"What the hell do you think I was getting at?" He stared down at her. "Why do you think I badgered Farkie into selling me that house? I was with him when he went through it after his mother died last December, and I didn't have the slightest interest in the place. It wasn't until you convinced me that we ought to live in the city that I suddenly remembered it. Why do you think I asked you to help me decide how to remodel it? When I think of what I went through trying to wrench a compromise out of you on that contract . . . Honestly, Libby, for a very intelligent woman you can be remarkably obtuse."

"Well, how was I supposed to know?" she defended herself. "I though Farkie's mother had just died. I didn't know the house had been empty all winter. And you could have been buying it as an investment. And as for that contract, it was your idea to negotiate as if we were serious and that's all it seemed like you were doing."

"In the beginning that's all I was doing. Oh, I was attracted to you the first time you barged into my apartment wearing that shapeless sweatshirt and breathing fire and brimstone. But it wasn't love. It was plain old-fashioned lust. You are one sexy lady, Liberty Joy Michalowski." He dropped a light kiss on her shiny nose.

"It wasn't until we'd started negotiating the contract that I began to realize what I felt for you went a lot deeper than merely being attracted to your surface beauty. By then, the fact that you looked like the reincarnation of every schoolboy's dream didn't seem so important as other facets of your personality. Your loyalty to your father, your compassion, the slightly off-center way you look at the world, the straightforward manner you attack problems. When I looked at you, I saw a woman unlike any I've ever met before. I knew you were my other half and . . ."

"Then why didn't you tell me how you felt?" Libby demanded.

"Because I was afraid to force the issue." He grimaced. "I felt that by postponing proposing, I'd be giving you more time to fall irrevocably in love with me. Besides, I didn't want you to have an unfair advantage in the negotiations."

"Speaking of negotiations, whatever happened to that contract?"

"The final version is safely locked in my office safe in case you try to renege."

A wild feeling of elation was racing through her veins. She didn't know how, but a miracle had happened. Joe loved her and wanted to marry her. Nothing else mattered.

"God, but I want to kiss you." He eyed her lips hungrily. "I've been starved for the taste and the feel and the smell of you this past week."

"Me, too," she admitted, pressing closer to him.

Joe put his hands on her shoulders and gently moved her back from him. "I don't think I'd better touch you until we're alone, because once I start, I'm not sure I'm going to be able to stop, and I've already done enough damage to your reputation." He glanced ruefully at the closed doors that led into the church.

Libby giggled. "You just livened things up a little, but I'd just as soon not meet those people again until something else has occurred to eclipse this afternoon's events."

"Our wedding will be soon enough to see them," he agreed, and Libby's heart swelled with joy at the thought. "But right now we're going to my place." He encircled her shoulders and pulled her to him as if he couldn't bare to let her go.

"To see your etchings?" she teased.

"To restore my sanity," he replied seriously. "After that, we'll go over to the house and see what they've accomplished while I was in Europe. After you left, I didn't have the heart to go by myself."

"I love you, Joe Landowski." Libby pressed close to his side for a second.

"And I love you, Liberty Joy Michalowski." His words were a vow. "First thing tomorrow morning, we're going to get a marriage license and visit your parish priest. Come on. Let's get out of here before we really give them something to talk about." He leaned against the heavy outside door, holding it open for her.

"Yes, let's." Libby took his hand as the door closed behind them.

"PERFECT." A satisfied sigh sounded from the shadows.

"Not bad if I do say so myself." Sigismund followed Frederic out into the center of the vestibule.

"Who would have thought that it would come to this?"

"Certainly not me," Casimir said frankly. "You have to admit, we got very lucky."

"Lucky, nothing!" Frederic protested. "It was sheer genius on our part."

"True," Sigismund agreed. "I've never seen such a clever trap as the one we baited."

"Agatha," Frederic inserted. The other two turned to loo
at him.

"What?" Casimir asked.

"Agatha," Frederic repeated. "For the name of my firs
granddaughter."

"Not Agatha!" Sigismund objected. "Not my grand
daughter. The kids will call her Aggie and an aggie is a mar
ble. Nobody's calling my granddaughter a marble."

"I can think of a few things to call you two," Casimir sai
in disgust.

"Alexandra." Sigismund paid no heed to him. "We'll cal
her Alexandra."

"Agatha!" Frederic glared at him.

"Champagne," Casimir said.

"Who ever heard of calling a girl champagne?" Frederi
demanded.

"I've heard of Brandy," Sigismund offered.

"Not to name, to drink," Casimir elaborated. "Suppose w
leave the naming of the kids to the parents and celebrate ou
success."

"Good idea." Sigismund beamed at him. "We'll drink t
their wedding."

"And to the grandchildren who'll brighten our old age,
Frederic added.

"What if they decide to wait a few years before they star
their family?" Sigismund came to a halt on the church step
as the horrible idea occurred to him.

"They won't," Frederic said, and then continued in les
emphatic tones, "and if they do, I have an idea. The three o
us could . . ."

"No!" Casimir interrupted. "Leave well enough alone. Be
sides, from what I saw, you two haven't anything to worry
about. They're besotted with each other."

"Yes." Frederic sighed happily. "They are, aren't they? W
really did pull it off. You know, maybe we ought to expand.

"Expand?" Sigismund asked as he hailed a taxi.

"Yes, expand. I've got this niece who's dying to get married and now that we've got the bugs worked out of the matchmaking business . . ."

"You mean now that we were lucky enough to escape unscathed—" Casimir followed the other two into the cab "—we're going to retire while we're still batting a thousand." He slammed the cab door shut behind them.

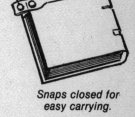

Take 4 books & a surprise gift FREE

SPECIAL LIMITED-TIME OFFER

Mail to   **Harlequin Reader Service**®

In the U.S.
901 Fuhrmann Blvd.
P.O. Box 1394
Buffalo, N.Y. 14240-1394

In Canada
P.O. Box 2800, Station "A"
5170 Yonge Street
Willowdale, Ontario M2N 6J3

YES! Please send me 4 free Harlequin Temptation® novels and my free surprise gift. Then send me 4 brand-new novels every month as they come off the presses. Bill me at the low price of $1.99 each—a 13% saving off the retail price. There are no shipping, handling or other hidden costs. There is no minimum number of books I must purchase. I can always return a shipment and cancel at any time. Even if I never buy another book from Harlequin, the 4 free novels and the surprise gift are mine to keep forever.   142-BPX-BP6S

Name _____ (PLEASE PRINT)

Address _____   Apt. No. _____

City _____ State/Prov. _____ Zip/Postal Code _____

This offer is limited to one order per household and not valid to present subscribers. Price is subject to change.   DOHT–SUB–1R